Puffin Books
DOLPHIN ISLAND

It is the twenty-first century. Johnny Clinton has stowed
away – almost by accident – on a giant hovership, the
Santa Anna. But his voyage nearly ends before it has even
started, when the *Santa Anna* is shipwrecked and Johnny
finds himself clinging to a makeshift raft in the dark,
somewhere in the South Pacific. For Johnny, this is just
the beginning of a very strange adventure involving
dolphins, killer whales, a hurricane and an underwater
conspiracy – and a great deal of excitement and danger.

Arthur C. Clarke was born in England in 1917, but has
lived in Sri Lanka since 1956. Author of forty books and
one of the most famous of science-fiction writers, he is
also well known for his screenplay for the film *2001: A
Space Odyssey*.

Arthur C. Clarke

Dolphin Island

A story of the People of the Sea

Illustrations by Robin Anderson

PUFFIN BOOKS

PUFFIN BOOKS

Published by the Penguin Group
Penguin Books Ltd, 27 Wrights Lane, London W8 5TZ, England
Penguin Books USA Inc., 375 Hudson Street, New York, New York 10014, USA
Penguin Books Australia Ltd, Ringwood, Victoria, Australia
Penguin Books Canada Ltd, 10 Alcorn Avenue, Toronto, Ontario, Canada M4V 3B2
Penguin Books (NZ) Ltd, 182–190 Wairau Road, Auckland 10, New Zealand

Penguin Books Ltd, Registered Offices: Harmondsworth, Middlesex, England

First published by Victor Gollancz Ltd 1963
Published in Puffin Books 1986
10 9 8 7 6 5

Printed in England by Clays Ltd, St Ives plc
Typeset in Linotype Plantin

One

Johnny Clinton was sleeping when the hovership raced down the valley, floating along the old turnpike on its cushion of air. The whistling roar in the night did not disturb him, for he had heard it almost all his life. To any boy of the twenty-first century, it was a sound of magic, telling of far-off countries and strange cargoes carried in the first ships that could travel with equal ease across land and sea.

No, the familiar roar of the air jets could not awaken him, though it might haunt his dreams. But now it had suddenly stopped, here in the middle of Transcontinental Thruway 21. That was enough to make Johnny sit up in bed, rubbing his eyes and straining his ears into the night. What could have happened? Had one of the great land-liners *really* halted here, four hundred miles from the nearest terminus?

Well, there was one way to find out. For a moment he hesitated, not wishing to face the winter cold. Then he plucked up his courage, wrapped a blanket around his shoulders, quietly eased up the window, and stepped out on to the balcony.

It was a beautiful, crisp night, with an almost full Moon lighting up every detail of the sleeping landscape. Johnny could not see the turnpike from the southern side of the house, but the balcony ran completely around the old-fashioned building, and it took him only seconds to tiptoe around to the northern face. He was especially careful to be quiet when passing the bedrooms of his aunt and cousins; he knew what would happen if he woke *them*.

But the house slept soundly beneath the winter Moon, and none of his unsympathetic relatives stirred as Johnny tiptoed past their windows. Then he forgot all about them, for he saw that he had not been dreaming.

The hovership had left the wide lane of the turnpike and, with lights blazing, lay on flat ground a few hundred yards to the side of the Thruway. Johnny guessed that it was a freighter, not a passenger liner, for there was only one observation deck, and that ran for only part of the vessel's five hundred feet of length. The ship looked, Johnny could not help thinking, exactly like a giant flat-iron – except that instead of a handle running lengthwise, there was a streamlined bridge crosswise, a third of the distance back from the bows. Above the bridge a red beacon was flashing on and off, warning any other craft that might come this way.

She must be in some kind of trouble, thought Johnny. I wonder how long she'll be here? Time for me to run down and have a good look at her? He had never seen a hovership at close quarters – at least, not one at rest. You didn't see much when they roared past at three hundred miles an hour.

It did not take him long to make up his mind. Ten minutes later, hurriedly dressed in his warmest clothes, he was quietly unbolting the back door. As he stepped out into the freezing night, he never dreamed that he was leaving the house for the last time. And even if he had known, he would not have been sorry.

Two

The closer Johnny approached it, the more enormous the hovership appeared. Yet it was not one of the giants like the hundred-thousand-ton oil or grain carriers that sometimes went whistling through the valley; it probably grossed only fifteen or twenty thousand tons. Across its bows it bore the words SANTA ANNA, BRASILIA in somewhat faded lettering. Even in the moonlight, Johnny had the distinct impression that the whole ship could do with a new coat of paint and a general clean up. If the engines were in the same state as the patched and shabby hull, that would explain this unscheduled halt.

There was not the slightest sign of life as Johnny circumnavigated the stranded monster. But this did not surprise him; freighters were largely automatic, and one this size was probably run by less than a dozen men. If his theory was correct, they would all be gathered in the engine room, trying to find what was wrong.

Now that she was no longer supported by her jets, the *Santa Anna* rested on the huge flat-bottomed buoyancy chambers that served to keep her afloat if she came down on the sea. They ran the full length of the hull, and as Johnny walked along them, they loomed above him like overhanging walls. In several places it was possible to scale those walls, for there were steps and handholds recessed into the hull, leading to entrance hatches about twenty feet from the ground.

Johnny looked thoughtfully at these openings. Of course, they were probably locked; but what would happen if he *did* go aboard? With any luck, he might have a good look around before the crew caught him and threw him out. It was the

chance of a lifetime, and he'd never forgive himself if he missed it . . .

He did not hesitate any longer, but started to climb the nearest ladder. About fifteen feet· from the ground he had second thoughts, and paused for a moment.

It was too late; the decision was made for him. Without any warning, the great curving wall to which he was clinging like a fly began to vibrate. A roaring howl, as of a thousand tornadoes, shattered the peaceful night. Looking down, Johnny could see dirt, stones, tufts of grass, being blasted outwards from beneath the ship as the *Santa Anna* hoisted herself laboriously into the air. He could not go back; the jets would blow him away like a feather in a gale. The only escape was upwards – and he had better get aboard before the ship started to move. What would happen if the hatch was locked he dared not imagine.

He was in luck. There was a handle, folded flush with the surface of the metal door, which opened inwards to reveal a dimly lit corridor. A moment later, heaving a great sigh of relief, Johnny was safely inside the *Santa Anna*. As he closed the door, the scream of the jets died to a muffled thunder – and at the same moment, he felt the ship beginning to move. He was on his way to an unknown destination.

For the first few minutes, he was scared; then he realized that there was nothing to worry about. He had only to find his way to the bridge, explain what had happened, and he'd be dropped off at the next stop. The police would get him home in a few hours.

Home. But he had no home; there was no place where he really belonged. Twelve years ago, when he was only four, both his parents had been killed in an air crash; ever since then he had lived with his mother's sister. Aunt Martha had a family of her own, and she had not been very pleased at the addition.

It had not been so bad while plump, cheerful Uncle James was alive, but now that he was gone, it had become more and more obvious to Johnny that he was a stranger in the house.

So why should he go back – at least, before he had to do so? This was a chance that would never come again, and the more he thought about it, the more it seemed to Johnny that Fate had taken charge of his affairs. Opportunity beckoned, and he would follow where it led.

His first problem would be to find somewhere to hide. That should not be difficult, in a vessel as large as this; but unfortunately he had no idea of the *Santa Anna*'s layout, and unless he was careful, he might blunder into one of the crew. Perhaps the best policy would be to look for the cargo section, for no one would be likely to go there while the ship was on the move.

Feeling very much like a burglar, Johnny began to explore, and was soon completely lost. He seemed to wander for miles, along dimly lit corridors and passageways, up spiral stairs and down vertical ladders, past hatches and doors bearing mysterious names. Once he ventured to open one of these when he found the sign, 'Main Engines', too much to resist. Very slowly, he pushed the metal door ajar and found himself looking down into a huge chamber almost filled with turbines and compressors. Great air ducts, thicker than a man, led from the ceiling and out through the floor, and the sound of a hundred hurricanes shrieked in his ears. The wall on the far side of the engine-room was covered with instruments and controls, and three men were examining these with such attention that Johnny felt quite safe in spying on them. In any case, they were more than fifty feet away from him, and would hardly notice a door that had been opened a couple of inches.

They were obviously holding a conference – mostly by signs, since it was impossible to talk in this uproar. Johnny soon realized that it was more of an argument than a conference, for there was much violent gesticulation, pointing to meters, and shrugging of shoulders. Finally, one of the men threw up his arms as if to say, 'I wash my hands of the whole business,' and stalked out of the engine-room. The *Santa Anna*, Johnny decided, was not a happy ship.

He found his hiding place a few minutes later. It was a small storage room, about twenty feet square, crammed with freight and baggage. When Johnny saw that every item was addressed to places in Australia, he knew that he would be safe until he was a long, long way from home. There would be no reason for anyone to come here until the ship had crossed the Pacific and was on the other side of the world.

Johnny clawed a small space among the crates and parcels, and sat down with a sigh of relief, resting his back against a large packing case labelled 'Bundaberg Chemical Pty'. He wondered what 'Pty' stood for, and still hadn't hit upon 'Proprietary' when excitement and exhaustion caught up with him, and he fell asleep on the hard metal floor.

When he awoke, the ship was at rest; he could tell this immediately because of the silence and the absence of all vibration. Johnny looked at his watch and saw that he had been aboard for five hours. In that time – assuming that she had made no other unscheduled stops – the *Santa Anna* could easily have travelled a thousand miles. Probably she had reached one of the great inland ports along the Pacific coast, and would be heading out to sea as soon as she had finished loading cargo.

If he was caught now, Johnny realized, his adventure would soon be ended. He had better stay where he was until the ship was on the move again, far out over the ocean. She would certainly not turn back to discharge a sixteen-year-old stowaway.

But he was hungry and thirsty; sooner or later he would have to get some food and water. The *Santa Anna* might be waiting here for days, and in that case he'd be starved out of his hiding place ...

11

He decided not to think about eating, though that was difficult because it was now his breakfast time. Great adventurers and explorers, Johnny told himself firmly, had suffered far worse hardships than this.

Luckily, the *Santa Anna* remained only an hour at this unknown port of call. Then, to his great relief, Johnny felt the floor start to vibrate and heard the distant shrilling of the jets. There was an unmistakable lifting sensation as the ship heaved herself off the ground, then a surge as she moved forward. In two hours, thought Johnny, he should be well out at sea – if his calculations had been correct and this was indeed the last stop on land.

He waited out the two hours as patiently as he could, then decided it was safe to give himself up. Feeling just a little nervous, he set off in search of the crew – and, he hoped, of something to eat.

But it was not as easy to surrender as he had expected; if the *Santa Anna* had appeared large from the outside, from the inside she seemed absolutely enormous. He was getting hungrier and hungrier – and had still seen no signs of life.

He did, however, find something that cheered him considerably. This was a small porthole, which gave him his first view of the outside world. It was not a very good view, but it was quite enough. As far as he could see, there was a grey, choppy expanse of waves. There was no sign of land – nothing but empty water, racing beneath him at a tremendous speed.

It was the first time that Johnny had ever seen the ocean. All his life he had lived far inland, among the hydroponic farms of the Arizona desert or the new forests of Oklahoma. To see so much wild and unconfined water was wonderful, and a little terrifying. He stood for a long time staring through the porthole, trying to grasp the fact that he was indeed racing away from the land of his birth, towards a country of which he knew nothing. It was certainly too late now to change his mind . . .

He found the answer to the food problem quite unexpectedly, when he stumbled upon the ship's lifeboat. It was a 25-foot, completely enclosed motor launch, tucked under a section of the hull that could be opened like a huge window. The boat was slung between two small cranes that could swing outwards to drop it in the sea.

Johnny could not resist climbing into the little boat – and the first thing he noticed was a locker marked 'Emergency Rations'. The struggle with his conscience was a brief one; thirty seconds later, he was nibbling biscuits and some kind of compressed meat. A tank of rather rusty water soon satisfied his thirst, and presently he felt much better. This was not going to be a luxury cruise, but its hardships would now be endurable.

This discovery made Johnny change his plans. There was no need to give himself up; he could hide for the whole duration of the trip – and, with any luck, he could walk off at the end without being spotted. What he would do afterwards he had no idea, but Australia was a big place, and he was sure that something would turn up.

Back in his hide-out, with enough food for the twenty hours that was the longest that the voyage could possibly last, Johnny tried to relax. Sometimes he dozed; sometimes he looked at his watch and tried to calculate where the *Santa Anna* must be. He wondered if she would stop at Hawaii or one of the other Pacific islands, and hoped that she would not. He was anxious to start his new life as quickly as possible.

Once or twice he thought of Aunt Martha. Would she be sorry that he had run away? He did not believe so, and he was sure that his cousins would be very happy to have got rid of him. One day, when he was rich and successful, he would contact them again, just for the satisfaction of seeing their faces. And that went for most of his classmates, too, *especially* those who made fun of his small size and called him 'Tiny'. He'd show them that brains and determination were more important than brawn . . . It was pleasant to lose himself in such fantasies, and from them he drifted slowly into sleep.

He was still asleep when the voyage ended. The explosion shook him awake instantly, and a few seconds later he felt the impact as the *Santa Anna* crashed into the sea. Then the lights went out, and he was left in total darkness.

Three

It was the first time in his life that Johnny had ever felt utter, unreasoning panic. His limbs had turned to jelly; he could hardly breathe for the weight that was pressing on his chest. It seemed that he was already drowning – as indeed he might soon be unless he could escape from this trap.

He had to find the way out, but he was surrounded by crates and packing cases, and soon lost all sense of direction as he blundered among them. It was like one of those nightmares when you tried to run and couldn't; but this was no dream – it was all too real.

The pain and shock of crashing against some unseen obstacle jarred him out of his panic. It was no good losing his head and stumbling around in the dark. The thing to do was to keep moving in the same direction until he found the wall. Then he could work along it until he came to the door.

The plan was excellent, but there were so many obstructions that it seemed an age before he felt smooth metal in front of him and knew that he had reached the wall of the compartment. After that, the rest was easy, and he almost cried with relief when he found the door and jerked it open. For the corridor outside was not, as he had feared, also in darkness. The main lights had failed, but a dim emergency system was operating, and he could see without difficulty.

It was then that he noticed the smell of smoke, and realized that the *Santa Anna* was on fire. He also noticed that the corridor was no longer level – the ship was badly down at the stern, where the engines were. Johnny guessed that the explosion had breached the hull, and that the sea was coming in.

Perhaps the ship was in no danger, but he could not be sure. He did not like the way she was listing, still less the ominous creaking of the hull. The helpless ship was rolling and pitching in a most unpleasant manner, and Johnny felt a sensation in the pit of his stomach that he guessed must be the first sign of seasickness. He tried to ignore it and to concentrate on the more important matter of staying alive.

If the ship was sinking, he had better find his way to the lifeboat as quickly as possible; that would be where everyone else would be heading. The crew would be surprised to find another passenger, and he hoped there would be enough room for him.

But where was the lifeboat section? He had been there only once, and though he was sure he could find his way if he had plenty of time, this was just what he lacked. Because he was in such a hurry, he took several wrong turnings and had to retrace his footsteps. Once he found his way blocked by a massive steel bulkhead which, he was certain, had not been there before. Smoke curled around its edges and Johnny could hear, quite distinctly, a steady crackling sound from the far side. He turned and ran as fast as he could, back along the dimly lit passageway.

He was exhausted and desperately frightened when he finally got back on the correct track. Yes, this was the right corridor — there would be a short flight of stairs at the end, and that would lead to the lifeboat section. He started to run, now that he was near his goal and had no need to conserve his strength.

His memory had not played him false. The stairs were there, just as he had expected. But the boat was gone.

The hull was wide open, and the davits were slung outwards with their empty pulley blocks waving as if to tantalize him. Through the huge gap that had been opened to pass the lifeboat, fierce gusts of wind were blowing, bringing flurries of spray. The taste of salt was already bitter in Johnny's mouth; soon he would know it only too well.

Sick at heart, he walked to the opening and looked out over the sea. It was night, but the Moon that had seen the beginning of his adventure still shone upon its ending. Only yards below, an angry sea was smashing against the side of the ship, and ever and again a wave came climbing up the hull and went swirling around his feet. Even if the *Santa Anna* was not shipping water elsewhere, she would soon be doing so here.

Somewhere, not far away, there was a muffled explosion, and the emergency lights flickered and died. They had served him just long enough, for he could never have found his way here in the darkness. But did it matter anyway? He was alone, in a sinking ship, hundreds of miles from land.

He peered out into the night, searching for some sign of the lifeboat, but the sea was empty. The launch could, of course, be standing by on the other side of the *Santa Anna*, and he would be unable to see it. This seemed the most likely explanation, for the crew would hardly have left the area while the ship was still afloat. Yet they had certainly wasted no time, so they must have known that the situation was serious. Johnny wondered if the *Santa Anna* was carrying a cargo of explosives or inflammables — and if so, just when it would go up.

A wave slapped against his face, blinding him with spray; even during these few minutes, the sea had crept appreciably higher. Johnny would not have believed that so large a ship could go down so quickly; but hoverships, of course, were very lightly built and were not designed for this sort of treatment. He guessed that the water would be level with his feet in about ten minutes.

He was wrong. Suddenly, without any warning, the *Santa Anna* checked her slow, regular wallow and gave a great lurch, like a dying animal trying to get to its feet for the last time. Johnny did not hesitate; some instinct told him that she was going down and that he had better get as far away as he could.

Bracing himself for the chill, he hit the water in a smooth, clean dive. Even as he went under, he was surprised to experience not cold, but warmth. He had forgotten that during these last few hours he had passed from winter into summer.

When he came to the surface, he started swimming with all his might, in his clumsy but effective overarm stroke. Behind him he heard monstrous gurglings and crashings, and a roaring sound as of steam escaping from a geyser. Abruptly, all these noises ceased; there was only the moaning of the wind and the hissing of the waves as they swept past him into the night. The tired old *Santa Anna* went down smoothly, without any fuss, and the backward suction that Johnny had feared never arrived.

When he was sure that it was all over, he started to tread water while he surveyed the situation, and the first thing that he saw was the lifeboat, less than half a mile away. He waved his arms and shouted at the top of his voice, but it was quite useless. The boat was already leaving; even had anyone been looking back, it was unlikely that he would have been spotted. And, of course, no one would have dreamed that there was another survivor to be picked up.

Now he was alone, beneath a yellow, westering Moon and the strange stars of the southern skies. He could float here for hours; the sea, he had already noticed was much more buoyant than the freshwater creeks in which he had learned to swim. But however long he stayed afloat, it would make no difference in the end. There was not one chance in a million that anybody would find him; his last hope had vanished with the departing lifeboat.

Something bumped into him, making him yelp with surprise and alarm. But it was only a piece of debris from the ship. The water around him, Johnny noticed, was full of floating objects. The discovery raised his spirits a little, for if he could make a raft, that would improve his chances considerably. Perhaps he might even drift to land, like those men who had ridden the Pacific currents on the famous *Kon-Tiki*, almost a century ago.

He began swimming towards the slowly swirling debris, and found that the sea had suddenly become much smoother. Oil oozing from the wreck had calmed the waves, which no longer hissed angrily, but rose and fell in sluggish undulations. At first their height had scared him, but now as he bobbed up and down with their passage, he found that they could do him no harm. Even in his present predicament, it was exciting to know that one could rise safely and effortlessly over the biggest wave.

Presently he was pushing his way among floating boxes, pieces of wood, empty bottles, and all sorts of small flotsam. None of this was any use to him; he wanted something big enough to ride on. He had almost given up all hope of finding it when he noticed a dark rectangle rising and falling in the swell, about fifty feet away.

When he reached it, he was delighted to find that it was a large packing-case. With some difficulty, he scrambled aboard and found that it could carry his weight. The raft was not very stable, and had a tendency to capsize, until Johnny spread himself flat across it; then it rode the waves with about three inches to spare. In the brilliant moonlight, Johnny could read the stencilled letters across which he was lying. They said: 'PLEASE STORE IN A COLD, DRY PLACE'.

Well, he was hardly dry, but he was certainly getting cold. The wind blowing across his wet clothes was making him feel uncomfortably chilly, but he would have to put up with this until the sun rose. He looked at his watch and was not surprised to see that it had stopped. Even so, the time it showed made no sense; then he remembered that he must have crossed many time zones since he stole aboard the ill-fated *Santa Anna*. By now, his watch would be at least six hours fast.

He waited, shivering on his little raft, watching the Moon go down and listening to the noises of the sea. Though he was worried, he was no longer badly frightened. He had had so many narrow escapes that he had begun to feel that nothing could harm him. Even though he had no food or water, he was safe for several days. He refused to think further ahead than that.

The Moon slid down the sky, and the night grew darker around him. As it did so, he saw to his astonishment that the sea was ablaze with floating particles of light. They flashed on and off like electric signs, and formed a luminous lane behind his drifting raft. When he dipped his hand in the water, fire seemed to flow from his fingers.

The sight was so wonderful that for a moment he forgot his danger. He had heard that there were luminous creatures in the sea, but he had never dreamed that they existed in such countless myriads. For the first time, he began to glimpse something of the wonder and mystery of the great element that covered three-quarters of the globe, and which now controlled his destiny.

The Moon touched the horizon, seemed to hover there for a moment, and then was gone. Above him the sky was ablaze with stars – the ancient ones of the old constellations, the brighter ones that had been put there by man in the fifty years since he had ventured into space. But none of these were as brilliant as the stars that flashed beneath the sea in such billions that the raft appeared to float upon a lake of fire.

Even when the Moon had set, it seemed ages before the first sign of dawn. Then Johnny saw a faint hint of light in the eastern sky, watched eagerly as it spread along the horizon, and felt his heart leap as the golden rim of the sun pushed up over the edge of the world. Within seconds, the stars of sky and sea had vanished as if they had never existed, and day had come.

He had barely time to savour the beauty of the dawn when he saw something that robbed the morning of all its hope. Heading straight towards him out of the west, with a speed and purpose that chilled his blood, were dozens of grey, triangular fins.

Four

As those fins sliced towards the raft, cutting through the water with incredible speed, Johnny thought of all the gruesome tales he had read about sharks and shipwrecked sailors. He drew himself up into as little space as possible, at the centre of the packing-case. It wobbled alarmingly, and he realized how small a push would be needed to turn it over. To his surprise, he felt little fear, only a kind of numbed regret and a hope that, if the worst came to the worst, it would all be over quickly. And it seemed a pity, too, that no one would ever know what had happened to him . . .

Then the water around the raft was full of sleek, grey bodies, switchbacking along the surface in a graceful roller-coaster motion. Johnny knew almost nothing about the creatures of the sea, but surely, sharks did not swim in this fashion. And these animals were breathing air, just as he was; he could hear them wheezing as they went by, and he caught glimpses of blowholes opening and closing. Why, of course – they were dolphins!

Johnny relaxed and no longer tried to hide himself in the middle of his raft. He had often seen dolphins in films or on television, and he knew that they were friendly, intelligent creatures. They were playing like children among the wreckage of the *Santa Anna*, butting at the floating debris with their streamlined snouts, making the strangest whistling and creaking noises as they did so. A few yards away, one had reared its head completely out of the water and was balancing a plank on its nose, like a trained animal in a circus act; it seemed to be saying to its companions, 'Look at me – see how clever I am!'

The strange, un-human but intelligent head turned towards Johnny, and the dolphin dropped its plaything with an unmistakable gesture of surprise. It sank back into the water, squeaking with excitement, and a few seconds later, Johnny was surrounded by glistening, inquisitive faces. They were smiling faces, too, for the mouths of the dolphins seemed to be frozen in a kind of fixed grin – one so infectious that Johnny found himself smiling back at them.

He no longer felt alone; now he had companionship, even though it was not human and could do nothing to help him. It was fascinating to watch the leathery, dove-grey bodies moving around him with such effortless ease as they hunted among the debris of the *Santa Anna*. They were doing this, Johnny soon

realized, purely out of playfulness and fun; they were more like lambs gambolling in a spring meadow than anything he had ever expected to find in the sea.

The dolphins continued to bob up and to look at him from time to time, as if making sure that he had not run away. They watched with great curiosity as he pulled off his sodden clothing and spread it to dry in the sun, and they seemed to be giving the matter careful thought when Johnny asked them solemnly, 'Well, what shall I do now?'

One answer to that question was obvious: he had to arrange some shelter from the tropical sun before it roasted him alive. Luckily, this problem was quickly solved; he was able to build a little wigwam from some pieces of driftwood, which he lashed together with his handkerchief and then covered with his shirt. When he had finished, he felt quite proud of himself, and hoped that his audience appreciated his cleverness.

Now he could do nothing but lie down in the shade and conserve his strength while the wind and the currents carried him to an unknown fate. He did not feel hungry, and though his lips were already dry, it would be several hours before thirst became a serious problem.

The sea was much calmer now, and low, oily waves were rolling past with a gentle, undulating motion. Somewhere Johnny had come across the phrase, 'Rocked in the cradle of the deep'. Now he knew exactly what it meant. It was so soothing, so peaceful here that he could almost forget his desperate position; he was content to stare at the blue sea and the blue sky, and to watch the strange yet beautiful animals that glided and swooped around him, sometimes hurling their bodies clear out of the water in the sheer joy of life ...

Something jolted the raft, and he awoke with a start. For a moment he could hardly believe that he had been sleeping and that the sun was now almost overhead. Then the raft jerked again – and he saw why.

Four dolphins, swimming side by side, were pushing the raft through the water. Already it was moving faster than a man could swim, and it was still gaining speed. Johnny stared in amazement at the animals splashing and snorting only inches away from him; was this another of their games?

Even as he asked himself that question, he knew that the answer was No. The whole pattern of their behaviour had changed completely; this was deliberate and purposeful. Playtime was over. He was in the centre of a great pack of the animals, all now moving steadily in the same direction. There were scores, if not hundreds, ahead and behind, to right and left, as far as he could see. He felt that he was moving across the ocean in the midst of a military formation – a brigade of cavalry.

He wondered how long they would keep it up, but they showed no signs of slackening. From time to time, one of the dolphins would drop away from the raft, and another would immediately take its place, so that there was no loss of speed. Though it was very hard to judge how fast he was moving, Johnny guessed that the raft was being pushed along at over five miles an hour. There was no way of telling, however, whether he was moving north, south, east, or west; he could get no compass bearings from the almost vertical sun.

Not until much later in the day did he discover that he was heading towards the west, for the sun was going down in front of him. He was glad to see the approach of night, and looked forward to its coolness after the scorching day. By this time he was extremely thirsty; his lips were parched and cracked, and though he was tantalized by the water all around him, he knew that it would be dangerous to drink it. His thirst was so over-powering that he did not feel any hunger; even if he had some food, he would be unable to swallow it.

It was a wonderful relief when the sun went down, sinking in a blaze of gold and red. Still the dolphins drove on into the west, beneath the stars and the rising Moon. If they kept this up all through the night, Johnny calculated, they would have carried him the best part of a hundred miles. They *must* have a definite goal, but what could it be? He began to hope that there was land not far away, and that for some unknown reason these friendly intelligent creatures were taking him to it. But why they were going to all this trouble he could not imagine.

The night was the longest that Johnny had ever known, for his growing thirst would not allow him to sleep. To add to his distress, he had been badly sunburned during the day, and he kept twisting and turning on the raft in a vain attempt to find

24

a comfortable position. Most of the time he lay flat on his back, using his clothes to protect the sore spots, while the Moon and stars crept across the sky with agonizing slowness. Sometimes the brilliant beacon of a satellite would drift from west to east, travelling much more swiftly than any of the stars, and in the opposite direction. It was maddening to know that up on the space stations were men and instruments that could easily locate him – if they bothered to search. But, of course, there was no reason why they should.

At last the Moon went down, and in the brief darkness before dawn the sea once more came alight with phosphorescence. The graceful, superbly streamlined bodies all around the raft were outlined with fire; every time one of them shot into the air, the trajectory of its leap was a glowing rainbow in the night.

This time Johnny did not welcome the dawn; now he knew how pitiful his defences were against the tropical sun. He re-erected his little tent, crept beneath it, and tried to turn his thoughts away from drink.

It was impossible. Every few minutes he found himself picturing cold milk-shakes, glasses of iced fruit juice, water flowing from fountains in sparkling streams. Yet he had been adrift for not more than thirty hours; men had survived without water for much longer than that.

The only thing that kept up his spirits was the determination and energy of his escort. The school still drove on into the west, carrying the raft before it with undiminished speed. Johnny no longer puzzled himself about the mystery of the dolphins' behaviour; that was a problem that would solve itself in good time – or not at all.

And then, about mid-morning, he caught his first glimpse of land. For many minutes he was afraid that it was merely a cloud on the horizon – but, if so, it was strange that it was the only cloud in the sky and that it lay dead ahead. Before long he could not doubt that it was an island, though it seemed to float clear of the water, and the heat-haze made its outlines dance and shimmer against the skyline.

An hour later, he could see its details clearly. It was long and low and completely covered with trees. A narrow beach of dazzling white sand surrounded it, and beyond the beach there seemed to be a very wide, shallow reef, for there was a line of white breakers at least a mile out at sea.

At first Johnny could see no signs of life, but at last, with great relief, he spotted a thin stream of smoke rising from the wooded interior. Where there was smoke there were human beings – and the water for which his whole body was now craving.

He was still several miles from the island when the dolphins gave him a bad shock; they were turning aside as if to by-pass the land that was now so close. Then Johnny understood what they were doing. The reef was too great an obstacle; they were going to outflank it and approach the island from the other side.

The detour took at least an hour, but Johnny's mind was at rest, now that he felt sure that he was nearing safety. As the raft and its untiring escort swung around to the western side of the island, he saw first a small group of boats at anchor, then some low white buildings, then a collection of huts with dark-skinned people moving among them. There was a fairly large community here, on this lonely speck in the Pacific.

Now at last the dolphins seemed a little hesitant, and Johnny got the impression that they were reluctant to go into the shallow water. They pushed the raft slowly past the anchored boats, then backed off as if to say, 'It's up to you now.'

Johnny felt an overwhelming impulse to say some words of

thanks, but his mouth was too dry for speech. So he stepped quietly off the raft, found himself in water only waist deep, and waded ashore.

There were people running along the beach towards him, but they could wait. He turned towards the lovely powerful creatures who had brought him on this incredible journey, and waved them a grateful farewell. Already they were turning back towards their home, in the deep water of the open sea.

Then something seemed to happen to his legs, and as the sand came up to hit him, dolphins, island, and everything else vanished from his consciousness.

Five

When Johnny awoke, he was lying on a low bed inside a very clean, white-walled room. A fan was spinning above his head, and light filtered in through a curtain-covered window. A cane chair, a small table, a chest-of-drawers, and a wash-basin completed the furniture. Even without the faint smell of disinfectant, he would have known that he was in a hospital.

He sat up in bed, and immediately yelped with pain. From head to foot, he seemed to be on fire. When he looked down at his body, it was an angry red, and patches of skin were peeling off in large flakes. He had already received some medical attention, for the worst places had been liberally covered with white ointment.

Johnny gave up the idea of moving, at least for the time being, and collapsed back into bed with another involuntary cry. At that moment the door opened, and an enormous woman came into the room. Her arms were like bolsters, and the rest of her was built on the same scale. She must have weighed at least two hundred and fifty pounds, yet she was not unhealthily fat – she was simply huge.

'Well, young man,' she said. 'What's all the noise? I never heard such a fuss about a little sunburn.'

A broad smile spread across her flat, chocolate-brown face, just in time to check Johnny's indignant answer. He managed a feeble grin in reply, and submitted while she took his pulse and temperature.

'Now,' she said, as she put away the thermometer, 'I'm going to send you to sleep, and when you wake up, all the pain will be gone. But before I do that, you'd better give me your address so we can telephone your family.'

Johnny stiffened, despite his burns. After going through all this, he was determined not to be sent home by the next boat.

'I haven't any family,' he said. 'There's no one I want to send a message to.'

The nurse's eyebrows rose a fraction of an inch.

'H'mm,' she said, in a sceptical tone of voice. 'Well, in that case, we'll give you your nightcap right away.'

'Just a minute,' pleaded Johnny. 'Please tell me where I am. Is this Australia?'

The nurse took her time in answering as she slowly poured a colourless fluid into a measuring-glass.

'Yes and no,' she said. 'This is Australian territory, though it's a hundred miles from the mainland. You're on an island in the Great Barrier Reef, and very lucky to have reached it. Here, swallow this – it doesn't taste too bad.'

Johnny made a face, but the nurse was speaking the truth.

As the medicine went down, he asked one more question.

'What's this place called?'

The huge nurse gave a chuckle that sounded like a small thunderstorm going by.

'*You* should know,' she said. The drug must have been very quick acting because Johnny barely caught her next words before he was unconscious.

'We call it Dolphin Island.'

*

The next time he woke up he felt a slight stiffness, but all the burning had gone. So had half his skin, and for the next few days he was moulting like a snake.

Nurse, who had informed him that her name was Tessie and that she came from the island of Tonga, watched approvingly while he ate a hearty meal of eggs, tinned meat, and tropical fruits. After that, he felt ready for anything and was anxious to start exploring at once.

'Don't be so impatient,' said Nurse Tessie, 'there's plenty of time.' She was going through a bundle of clothing, hunting for shorts and shirt that would fit Johnny. 'Here, try these for size. And take this hat, too. Keep out of the sun until you've worked up a proper tan. If you don't, you'll be back here again, and that would make me very angry.'

'I'll be careful,' promised Johnny. He decided that it would be an extremely bad idea to make Nurse angry.

She put two fingers in her mouth and blew a piercing whistle, whereupon a tiny girl appeared almost instantly.

'Here's your dolphin-boy, Annie,' said Nurse. 'Take him to the office – Doctor's waiting.'

Johnny followed the child along paths of crushed coral fragments, blindingly white in the fierce sun. They wandered between large shady trees, which looked rather like oaks, except that their leaves were several sizes too big. Johnny was a little disappointed by this; he had always believed that tropical islands were covered with palms.

Presently the narrow road opened into a large clearing, and Johnny found himself looking at a group of single-storeyed concrete buildings, linked together with covered walks. Some had large windows behind which people could be seen at work; others had no windows at all and looked as if they contained machines, for pipes and cables led into them.

Johnny followed his little guide up the steps into the main building. As he walked past the windows, he could see the people inside staring at him curiously. That was not surprising, in view of the way he had arrived here. Sometimes he wondered if that strange ride was all imagination – it seemed too fantastic to be true. And was this place *really* called Dolphin Island, as Nurse Tessie had said? That would be an altogether outrageous coincidence.

His guide, who had apparently been too shy or too overawed to utter a word, disappeared as soon as she had led Johnny to a door marked 'Dr Keith – Assistant Director'. He knocked, waited until a voice said 'Come in', and pushed his way into a large air-conditioned office, refreshingly cool after the heat outside.

Dr Keith was a man in his forties, and looked like a college professor. Even though he was sitting behind his desk, Johnny could see that he was unusually tall and gangling; he was also the first white person he had seen on the island.

The doctor waved Johnny to a chair, saying in a slightly nasal voice as he did so, 'Sit down, sonny.'

Johnny didn't like being called 'sonny', nor did he like the doctor's Australian accent, which he had never before encountered at close quarters. But he said, 'Thank you', very politely, sat down, and waited for the next move.

It was completely unexpected. 'Perhaps you'd better begin

by telling us,' said Dr Keith, 'just what happened to you – after the *Santa Anna* went down.'

Johnny stared at him open-mouthed, all his plans in ruins. They had been only half-formed plans, but he had at least hoped that he could pose for a little while as a shipwrecked sailor suffering from loss of memory. But if they knew how he had travelled, they also knew where he had come from, and he would undoubtedly be sent home at once.

He decided not to give up without a fight.

'I've never heard of the *Santa*— whatever her name is,' he replied innocently.

'Give us credit for a little intelligence, sonny. When you came ashore in such a novel manner, we naturally radioed the coast guard to find if any ships had been lost. They told us that the crew of the hover-freighter *Santa Anna* had put in at Brisbane, reporting that their ship had sunk about a hundred miles east of us. However, they also reported that everyone had been saved, even the ship's cat.

'So that seemed to rule out the *Santa Anna*, until we had the bright idea that you might be a stowaway. After that, it was just a matter of checking with the police along the *Santa Anna*'s route.' The doctor paused for a moment, picked up a briar pipe from his desk, and examined it as if he'd never seen such an object before. It was at this point that Johnny decided that Dr Keith was just playing with him, and his initial dislike went up a few more degrees.

'You'd be surprised how many boys still run away from home,' continued that annoying voice. 'It took several hours to find out who you were – and I must say that when we called your Aunt Martha, she didn't sound particularly grateful. I don't really blame you for clearing out.'

Perhaps Dr Keith wasn't so bad after all. 'What are you going to do with me, now I'm here?' asked Johnny. He realized, to his alarm, that there was a slight quiver in his voice and that tears of disappointment and frustration were not far away.

'There's not much that we *can* do at the moment,' said the doctor, raising Johnny's hopes at once. 'Our boat's over at the mainland and won't be back until tomorrow. It will be a week after that before it sails again, so you have eight days here that you can count on.'

Eight days! His luck was still holding out. Many things could happen in that time – and he would make sure that they did.

In the next half-hour, Johnny described his ride back from the wreck while Dr Keith made notes and asked questions. Nothing about the story seemed to surprise him, and when Johnny had finished, he pulled a sheaf of photographs out of his desk drawer. They were pictures of dolphins; Johnny had no idea that there were so many different varieties.

'Could you identify your friends?' the doctor asked.

'I'll try,' said Johnny, riffling through the prints. He quickly eliminated all but three probables and two possibles.

Dr Keith looked quite satisfied with his choice of dolphins.

'Yes,' he said, 'it would have to be one of those.' Then he asked Johnny a very odd question.

'Did any of them speak to you?'

At first Johnny thought he was joking; then he saw that Dr Keith was perfectly serious.

'They made all sorts of noises – squeaks and whistles and barks – but nothing that I could understand.'

'Nothing like this?' asked the doctor. He pressed a button on his desk, and from a loud-speaker at the side of the office came a sound like a rusty gate creaking on its hinges. Then there was a string of noises that reminded Johnny of an old-fashioned gas engine starting up, and, after that, clearly and unmistakably, 'Good morning, Doctor Keith.'

The words were spoken more quickly than a man could utter them, but they were perfectly distinct. And even then, on that first hearing, Johnny knew that he was not listening to a mere echo or a parrot-like repetition. The animal that said, 'Good morning, Doctor Keith,' had known exactly what it was doing.

'You seem surprised,' chuckled the doctor. 'Hadn't you heard that dolphins could speak?'

Johnny shook his head.

'Well, it's been known for half a century that they have an elaborate language of their own. We've been trying to learn it – and, at the same time, trying to teach them Basic English. We've made a good deal of progress, thanks to the techniques worked out by Professor Kazan. You'll meet him when he comes back from the mainland; he's very anxious to hear your story. Meanwhile I'd better find someone to look after you.'

Dr Keith pressed a switch, and a reply came at once from an intercom speaker.

'School here. Yes, Doctor?'

'Any of the older boys free at the moment?'

'You can have Mick – and welcome to him.'

'Good – send him around to the office.'

Johnny sighed. Even on an island as small and remote as this, it seemed that one couldn't escape from school.

Six

As a guide to the island, Mick Nauru had just one drawback – he would exaggerate. Most of his tall stories were so outrageous that there was no danger of taking them seriously, but sometimes Johnny was left in doubt. Was it really true, for instance, that Nurse Tessie (or Two-Ton Tessie as the islanders called her) had left home because the *big* girls on Tonga poked fun at her for being so small? Johnny didn't think so, but Mick assured him that it was perfectly true. 'Ask her if you don't believe me,' he said, his face completely solemn beneath his huge mop of black, frizzy hair.

Luckily, his other information was more easily checked, and on matters that were really important, he was quite serious. As soon as Dr Keith had handed Johnny over to him, Mick took him on a quick tour of the island and introduced him to its geography.

There was quite a lot in a small area, and it was several days before Johnny knew his way around. The first thing he learned was that Dolphin Island had two populations – the scientists and technicians of the research station, and the fisherfolk who operated the boats and made a living from the sea. The fishing community also provided the workers who ran the power station, water supply, and other essential services, such as the cookhouse, laundry, and the tiny farm of ten pampered cows.

'We brought in the cows,' explained Mick, 'after the Professor tried to process dolphin milk. That's the only time we've ever had a mutiny on the island.'

'How long have you been here?' asked Johnny. 'Were you born here?'

'Oh, no, my people come from Darnley Island, up in the Torres Strait. They moved here five years ago, when I was twelve. The pay was good, and it sounded interesting.'

'And is it interesting?'

'You bet! I wouldn't go back to Darnley, or the mainland either. Wait until you see the reef, and you'll understand why.'

They had left the cleared paths and were taking a short-cut through the small forest which covered most of the island. Though the trees were closely packed, it was not hard to push a way through them, for there were none of the thorns and creepers that John had expected in a tropical forest. The plant life of the island was wild, but well behaved.

Some of the trees appeared to have small piles of sticks propped around their bases, and it was some time before Johnny realized that the props were actually part of the trees. It seemed that they did not trust the soft soil in which they were growing, and had sent out extra roots above ground as buttresses.

'They're pandanus,' explained Mick. 'Some people call them bread-fruit trees, because you can make a kind of bread from them. I ate some once; it tasted horrible. Look out!'

He was too late. Johnny's right leg had sunk into the ground up to his knee, and as he floundered to extricate himself, the left leg plunged even deeper.

'Sorry,' said Mick, who didn't look at all sorry. 'I should have warned you. There's a muttonbird colony here – they make their nests in the ground, like rabbits, and in some places you can't walk a foot without falling into them.'

'Thank you for telling me,' said Johnny sarcastically, as he clambered out and dusted himself off. There were a great many things to learn, it seemed, on Dolphin Island.

He came to grief several times in the burrows of the muttonbirds – or wedge-tailed shearwaters, to give them their proper name – before they emerged from the trees and walked down on to the beach on the eastern side of the island, facing the great emptiness of the open Pacific. It was hard to believe that he had come from far beyond that distant horizon, brought here by a miracle he still did not understand.

There was no sign of human life; they might have been the only inhabitants. This coast was exposed to the seasonal gales, so all the buildings and dock installations were on the opposite side of the island. A huge tree trunk, cast up on the sand and bleached white by months and years of sun, was a silent monument to some past hurricane. There were even great boulders of dead coral, weighing many tons, which could only have been hurled up on to the beach by wave action. And yet it all looked so peaceful now.

The boys started to walk along the sand dunes between the edge of the forest and the coral-covered beach. Mick was searching, and presently he found what he was looking for.

Something large had crawled up out of the sea, leaving what looked like tank tracks in the sand. At the end of the tracks, high above the water-level, there was an area of flattened sand in which Mick commenced to dig with his hands.

Johnny helped him, and about a foot down they came across dozens of eggs the size and shape of table-tennis balls. They were not hard shelled, however, but leathery and flexible. Mick took off his shirt, made a bag out of it, and packed in all the eggs he could.

'D'ya know what they are?' he asked.

'Yes,' said Johnny promptly, to Mick's obvious disappointment. 'Turtle eggs. I saw a film on television once, showing how the baby turtles hatch and then dig themselves out of the sand. What are you going to do with these?'

'Eat them, of course. They're fine, fried with rice.'

'Ugh!' said Johnny. 'You won't catch me trying it.'

'You won't know,' answered Mick. 'We've got a very clever cook.'

They followed the curve of the beach around the north of the island, then the west, before coming back to the settlement. Just before they reached it, they encountered a large pool, or tank, connected to the sea by a canal. As the tide was now out, the canal was closed by a lock gate, which trapped water in the pool until the sea returned.

'There you are,' said Mick. 'That's what the island is all about.'

Swimming slowly around in the pool, just as he had seen them out in the Pacific, were two dolphins. Johnny wished he could have examined them more closely, but a wire-mesh fence made it impossible to get near the pool. On the fence, in large red letters, was a message which read: QUIET PLEASE – HYDRO-PHONES IN ACTION.

They tiptoed dutifully past, then Mick explained: 'The Prof doesn't like anyone talking near the dolphins, says it's liable to confuse them. One night some crazy fisherman got drunk, and came and shouted a lot of bad language at them. There was an awful row – he was chucked out on the next boat.'

'What sort of man is the Prof?' asked Johnny.

'Oh, he's fine – except on Sunday afternoons.'

'What happens then?'

'Every Sunday morning his old lady calls and tries to talk him into coming home. He won't go, says he hates Moscow – it's too hot in the summer and too cold in the winter. So they have terrific fights, but every few months they compromise and meet at somewhere like Yalta.'

Johnny thought this over. He was anxious to learn all that he could about Professor Kazan, in the hope of improving his chances of staying on the island. Mick's description sounded a little alarming; still, as Sunday had just passed, the Professor should be in a good temper for several days.

'Can he *really* talk dolphin language?' asked Johnny. 'I didn't think anyone could imitate those weird noises.'

'He can't speak more than a few words, but he can translate tape recordings, with the help of computers. And then he can make new tapes and talk back to them. It's a complicated business, but it works.'

Johnny was impressed, and his curiosity was aroused. He had always liked to know how things worked, and he couldn't imagine how one would even begin to learn dolphin language.

'Well,' said Mick, when he put the question to him, 'have you ever stopped to think how *you* learned to speak?'

'By listening to my mother, I suppose,' Johnny answered, a little sadly; he could just remember her.

'Of course. So what the Prof did was to take a mother dolphin with a new baby, and put them into a pool by themselves.

Then he listened to the conversation as the baby grew up; that way, he learned Dolphin, just as the baby did.'

'It sounds almost too easy,' said Johnny.

'Oh, it took years, and he's still learning. But now he has a vocabulary of thousands of words, and he's even started to write Dolphin History.'

'History?'

'Well, you can call it that. Because they don't have books, they've developed wonderful memories. They can tell us about things that happened in the sea ages ago – at least, that's what the Prof says. And it makes sense; before men invented writing, they had to carry everything in their own heads. The dolphins have done the same.'

Johnny pondered these surprising facts until they had reached the administrative block and completed the circuit of the island. At the sight of all these buildings, housing so many busy workers and complicated machines, he was struck by a more down-to-earth thought.

'Who pays for all this?' he asked. 'It must cost a fortune to run.'

'Not much, compared to the money that goes into space,' Mick answered. 'The Prof started fifteen years ago with about six helpers. When he began getting results, the big science foundations gave him all the support he needed. So now we have to tidy the place up every six months for a lot of fossils who call themselves an inspection committee. I've heard the Prof say it was much more fun in the old days.'

That might be true, thought Johnny. But it looked as if it was still a lot of fun now – and he intended to share it.

Seven

The hydrofoil launch *Flying Fish* came scudding out of the west at fifty knots, making the crossing from the Australian mainland in two hours. When she was near the Dolphin Island reef, she retracted her huge water-skis, settled down like a conventional boat, and finished her journey at a sedate ten knots.

Johnny knew that she was in sight when the whole population of the island started to migrate down to the jetty. He followed out of curiosity, and stood watching on the beach as the white-painted launch came cautiously down the channel blasted through the coral.

Professor Kazan, wearing a spotlessly white tropical suit and a wide-brimmed hat, was the first ashore. He was warmly greeted by a reception committee in which technicians, fishermen, clerical staff and children were all mixed up together. The island community was extremely democratic, everyone regarding himself as the equal of everyone else. But Professor Kazan, as Johnny soon discovered, was in a class of his own, and the islanders treated him with a curious mixture of respect, affection and pride.

Johnny also discovered that if you came down to the beach to watch the *Flying Fish* arrive, you were expected to help unload her. For the next hour, he assisted an impressive flow of parcels and packing cases on its way from boat to 'Stores'. The job had just been finished, and he was having a welcome cool drink, when the public address system asked him if he would kindly report to Tech Block as soon as possible.

When he arrived, he was shown into a large room full of

electronic equipment. Professor Kazan and Dr Keith were sitting at an elaborate control desk, and took no notice of him at all. Johnny didn't mind; he was too fascinated at what was going on.

A strange series of sounds, repeated over and over again, was coming from a loud-speaker. It was like the dolphin noises that Johnny had already heard, but there was a subtle difference. After about a dozen repeats, he realized what this was. The sounds had been slowed down considerably, to allow sluggish human ears to appreciate their fine details.

But this was not all. Each time the string of dolphin noises came from the speaker, it also appeared as a pattern of light and shade on a large television screen. The pattern of bright lines and dark bands looked like a kind of map, and though it meant nothing to Johnny's untrained eye, it obviously conveyed a good deal to the scientists. They watched it intently every time it flashed on the screen, and occasionally they adjusted controls that brightened some areas and darkened others.

Suddenly, the Professor noticed Johnny, turned off the sound, and swivelled around in his seat. However, he did not switch off the picture, which continued flashing silently and steadily with such hypnotic rhythm that Johnny's eyes kept coming back to it.

All the same, he made the most of this first opportunity of studying Professor Kazan. The scientist was a plump, grey-haired man in his late fifties; he had a kindly but rather distant expression, as if he wanted to be friends with everyone, yet preferred to be left with his own thoughts. As Johnny was to discover, he could be excellent company when he relaxed, but at other times he would seem to be somewhere else altogether, even when he was talking to you. It was not that he bore much resemblance to the 'absent-minded professor' of the popular imagination; no one could be less absent-minded than Professor Kazan when it came to dealing with practical matters. He seemed to be able to operate on two levels at once: part of his mind would be coping with the affairs of every-day life, and another part would be wrestling with some profound scientific problem. No wonder, therefore, that he often appeared to be listening to some inner voice that no one else could hear.

'Sit down, Johnny,' he began. 'Dr Keith radioed about you while I was over on the mainland. I suppose you realize just how lucky you've been?'

'Yes, sir,' answered Johnny, with considerable feeling.

'We've known for centuries that dolphins sometimes help humans to shore – in fact, such legends go back for over two thousand years, though no one took them very seriously until our time. But you weren't merely pushed to land; you were carried a hundred miles.

'On top of that, you were brought directly to *us*. But why? This is what we'd very much like to know. I don't suppose you have any ideas?'

Johnny was flattered by the question, but could do little to answer it.

'Well,' he said slowly, 'they must have known that you were working with dolphins, though I can't imagine how they found out.'

'That's easy to answer,' Dr Keith interjected. 'The dolphins we've released must have told them. Remember, Johnny recognized five of them from photographs I showed him when he first arrived.'

Professor Kazan nodded.

'Yes – and that gives us some valuable information. It means that the coastal species we work with and their deep-sea cousins speak the same language. We didn't know *that* before.'

'But we're still in the dark about their motives,' said Dr Keith. 'If wild dolphins that have never had any direct contact

43

with men go to all this trouble, it suggests that they want some-thing from us – and want it badly. Perhaps rescuing Johnny meant something like, "We've helped you – now help us." '

'It's a plausible theory,' agreed Professor Kazan. 'But we won't find the answer by talking. There's only one way to dis-cover what Johnny's friends were driving at – and that's to ask them.'

'*If* we can find them.'

'Well, if they really want something, they won't be too far away. We may be able to contact them without leaving this room.'

The Professor threw a switch, and once more the air was full of sound. But this time, Johnny soon realized, he was not listening to the voice of a single dolphin, but to all the voices of the sea.

It was an incredibly complex mixture of hissings and crack-lings and rumblings. Mingled with these, there were chirps that might have been made by birds, faint and distant moans, and the murmur of a million waves.

They listened for several minutes to this fascinating medley of noises; then the Professor turned another switch on the huge machine.

'That was Hydrophone West,' he explained to Johnny. 'Now we'll try Hydro East. It's in deeper water, right off the edge of the Reef.'

The sound picture changed; the noise of the waves was fainter, but the moanings and creakings from the unknown creatures of the sea were much louder. Once more the Profes-sor listened for several minutes, then he switched to North, and finally to South.

'Run the tapes through the analyser, will you?' he asked Dr Keith. 'But I'd be willing to bet, even now, that there's no large school of dolphins within twenty miles.'

'In that case, bang goes my theory.'

'Not necessarily; twenty miles is nothing to dolphins. And they're hunters, remember, so they can't stay in one place. They have to follow their food wherever it goes. The school that rescued Johnny would soon vacuum-clean all the fish off our reef.'

The Professor rose to his feet, then continued:

'I'll leave you to run the analysis; it's time I went down to the pool. Come along, Johnny, I want you to meet some of my best friends.'

As they walked towards the beach, the Professor seemed to fall into a reverie. Then he startled Johnny by suddenly and skilfully producing a string of rapidly modulated whistles.

He laughed at Johnny's surprised expression.

'No human being will ever speak fluent Dolphin,' he said, 'but I can make a fair attempt at a dozen of the commoner phrases. I have to keep working at them, though, and I'm afraid my accent's pretty terrible. Only dolphins that know me well can understand what I'm trying to say. And sometimes I think they're just being polite.'

The Professor unlocked the gate to the pool, and then carefully locked it behind him.

'Everyone wants to play with Susie and Sputnik, but I can't allow it,' he explained. 'At least, not while I'm trying to teach them English.'

Susie was a sleek, excited matron of some three hundred pounds, who reared herself half out of the water as they approached. Sputnik, her nine-month-old son, was more reserved, or perhaps more shy; he kept his mother between himself and the visitors.

'Hello, Susie,' said the Professor, speaking with exaggerated clarity. 'Hello, Sputnik.' Then he pursed his lips and let fly with that complicated whistle. Something went wrong half-way through, and he swore softly under his breath before going back to start afresh.

Susie thought this was very funny. She gave several yelps of dolphin laughter, then squirted a jet of water at her visitors, though she was polite enough to miss them. Then she swam up to the Professor, who reached into his pocket and produced a plastic bag full of titbits.

He held one piece high in the air, whereupon Susie backed away a few yards, came shooting out of the water like a rocket, took the food neatly from the Professor's fingers, and dived back into the pool with scarcely a splash. Then she emerged again and said distinctly, 'Thank you, 'fessor.'

She was obviously waiting for more, but Professor Kazan shook his head.

'No, Susie,' he said, patting her on the back. 'No more; food-time soon.'

She gave a snort that seemed to express disgust, then went racing around the pool like a motor-boat, clearly showing off.

As Sputnik followed her, the Professor said to Johnny:

'See if you can feed him – I'm afraid he doesn't trust me.'

Johnny took the titbit, which smelled to high heaven of fish, oil, and chemicals. It was, he found later, the dolphin equivalent of tobacco or candy. The Professor had concocted it only after years of research; the animals loved the stuff so much that they would do almost anything to earn some.

Johnny knelt at the edge of the pool and waved the bait.

'Sputnik!' he called. 'Here, Sputnik!'

The little dolphin reared out of the water and regarded him doubtfully. It looked at its mother, it looked at Professor Kazan and then again at Johnny. Though it appeared tempted, it would not approach him; instead, it gave a snort and promptly submerged, after which it started tearing around in the depths of the pool. It did not seem to be going anywhere in particular;

like some human beings who cannot make up their minds, it was simply galloping off in all directions.

I think it's afraid of the Professor, Johnny decided. He walked along the edge of the pool until he had put fifty feet between himself and the scientist, then called to Sputnik again.

His theory worked. The dolphin surveyed the new situation, approved of it, and swam slowly towards Johnny. It still looked a little suspicious as it raised its snout and opened its mouth, displaying an alarming number of small but needle-sharp teeth. Johnny felt distinctly relieved when it took the reward without nipping his fingers. After all, Sputnik was a carnivore, and Johnny would not care to feed a half-grown lion cub with his bare hands.

The young dolphin hovered at the edge of the pool, obviously waiting for more. 'No, Sputnik,' said Johnny, remembering the Professor's words to Susie. 'No, Sputnik – food-time soon.'

The dolphin remained only inches away, so Johnny reached out to stroke it. Though it shied a little, it did not withdraw, but permitted him to run his hand along its back. He was surprised to find that the animal's skin was soft and flexible, like rubber; nothing could have been more unlike the scaly body of a fish; and no one who stroked a dolphin could ever again forget that it was a warm-blooded mammal.

Johnny would have liked to remain playing with Sputnik, but the Professor was signalling to him. As they walked away from the pool, the scientist remarked jokingly, 'My feelings are quite hurt. I've never been able to get near Sputnik – and you did it the first time. You seem to have a way with dolphins; have you ever kept any pets before?'

'No, sir,' said Johnny. 'Except polywogs, and that was a long time ago.'

'Well,' the Professor chuckled, 'I don't think we can count *them*.'

47

They had walked on for a few more yards, when Professor Kazan started speaking in a completely different tone of voice, addressing Johnny very seriously as an equal, not as a boy forty years younger.

'I'm a scientist,' he said, 'but I'm also a superstitious Russian peasant. Though logic tells me it's nonsense, I'm beginning to think that Fate sent you here. First, there was the way you arrived, like something out of a Greek myth. And now Sputnik feeds out of your hands. Pure coincidence, of course, but a sensible man makes coincidences work for him.'

What on earth is he driving at? wondered Johnny. But the Professor said no more until they were about to re-enter the Tech Block. Then he suddenly remarked, with a slight chuckle, 'I understand that you're in no great hurry to get home.'

Johnny's heart skipped a beat.

'That's right, sir,' he said eagerly. 'I want to stay here as long as I can. I'd like to learn more about your dolphins.'

'Not *mine*,' corrected the Professor firmly. 'Every dolphin is a person in his own right, an individual with more freedom than we can ever know on land. They don't belong to anyone, and I hope they never will. I want to help them, not only for Science, but because it's a privilege to do so. Never think of them as animals; in their language they call themselves the People of the Sea, and that's the best name for them.'

It was the first time that Johnny had seen the Professor so animated, but he could understand his feelings. For he owed his life to the People of the Sea, and it was a debt he hoped he could repay.

Eight

Around Dolphin Island lay a magic kingdom, the reef. In a lifetime, one could not exhaust its marvels. Johnny had never dreamed that such places existed, crammed with weird and beautiful creatures in such multitudes that the fields and forests of the land seemed dead by comparison.

At high tide, the reef was completely covered by the sea, and only the narrow belt of white sand surrounding the island was left exposed. But a few hours later, the transformation was incredible. Though the range between high and low tide was only three feet, the reef was so flat that the water withdrew for miles. Indeed, in some directions the tide retreated so far that the sea disappeared from sight, and the coral plateau was uncovered all the way to the horizon.

This was the time to explore the reef; all the equipment needed was a stout pair of shoes, a broad-brimmed hat to give protection from the sun, and a face mask. The shoes were far and away the most important item, for the sharp, brittle coral could inflict scars that easily became infected, and then took weeks to heal.

The first time that Johnny went out on to the reef, Mick was his guide. Because he had no idea what to expect, everything was very strange – and a little frightening. He did well to be cautious until he knew his way around. There were things on the reef – small, innocent-looking things – that could easily kill him if he was careless.

The two boys walked straight out from the beach on the western side of the island, where the exposed reef was only half a mile wide. At first they crossed an uninteresting no-man's land of dead, broken coral – shattered fragments cast up by the storms of centuries. The whole island was built of such fragments, which the ages had covered with a thin layer of earth, then with grass and weeds, and at last with trees.

They were soon beyond the zone of dead coral, and it seemed to Johnny that he was moving through a garden of strange, petrified plants. There were delicate twigs and branches of coloured stone, and more massive shapes like giant mushrooms or fungi, so solid that it was safe to walk on them. Yet despite their appearance, these were not plants, but the creations of animal life. When Johnny bent down to examine them, he could see that their surfaces were pierced by thousands of tiny holes. Each was the cell of a single coral polyp – a little creature like a small sea anemone – and each cell had been built of lime secreted by the animal during its lifetime. When it died, the empty cell would remain, and the next generation would build upon it. And so the reef would grow, year by year, century by century. Everything that Johnny saw – the miles upon miles of flat tableland, glistening beneath the sun – was the work of creatures smaller than his fingernail.

And this was only one patch of coral in the whole immensity of the Great Barrier Reef, which stretched for more than a thousand miles along the Australian coast. Now Johnny understood a remark that he had heard Professor Kazan make – that the Reef was the mightiest single work of living creatures on the face of the Earth.

It did not take Johnny long to discover that he was walking on other creatures besides corals. Suddenly, without the slightest warning, a jet of water shot into the air, only a few feet in front of him.

'Whatever did that?' he gasped.

Mick laughed at his amazement.

'Clam,' he answered briefly. 'It heard you coming.'

Johnny caught the next one in time to watch it in action. The clam was about a foot across, embedded vertically in the coral so that only its open lips were showing. The body of the creature (partly out of its shell), looked like a beautifully coloured piece of velvet, dyed the richest of emeralds and blues. When Mick stamped on the rock beside it, the clam instantly snapped shut in alarm – and the water it shot upward just missed Johnny's face.

'This is only a little feller,' said Mick contemptuously. 'You have to go deep to find the big ones – they grow up to four, five feet across. My grandfather says that when he was working on a pearling lugger from Cooktown, he met a clam twelve feet across. But he's famous for his tall stories, so I don't believe it.'

Johnny didn't believe in the five-foot clams either; but, as he found later, this time Mick was speaking the exact truth. It wasn't safe to dismiss *any* story about the reef and its creatures as pure imagination.

They had walked another hundred yards, accompanied by occasional squirts from annoyed clams, when they came to a small rock-pool. Because there was no wind to ruffle the surface, Johnny could see the fish darting through the depths as clearly as if they had been suspended in air.

They were all the colours of the rainbow, patterned in stripes and circles and spots as if some mad painter had run amok with his palette. Not even the most garish butterflies were more colourful and striking than the fish flitting in and out of the corals.

And the pool held many other inhabitants. When Mick pointed them out to him, Johnny saw two long feelers protruding from the entrance of a little cave; they were waving anxiously to and fro as if making a survey of the outside world.

'Painted Crayfish,' said Mick. 'Maybe we'll catch him on the way back. They're very good eating – barbecued with lots of butter.'

In the next five minutes, he had shown Johnny a score of different creatures. There were several kinds of beautifully patterned shells; five-armed starfish crawling slowly along the bottom in search of prey; hermit crabs hiding in the shells that they had made their homes; and a thing like a giant slug, which squirted out a cloud of purple ink when Mick prodded it.

There was also an octopus, the first that Johnny had ever seen. It was a baby, a few inches across, and it was lurking shyly in the shadows, where only an expert like Mick could have spotted it. When he scared it out into the open, it slithered over the corals with a graceful flowing motion, changing its colour from dull grey to a delicate pink as it did so. Much to his surprise, Johnny decided that it was quite a pretty little creature, though he expected that he would change his views if he met a really large specimen.

He could have spent all day exploring this one small pool, but Mick was in a hurry to move along. So they continued their trek towards the distant line of the sea, zigzagging to avoid areas of coral too fragile to bear their weight.

Once, Mick stopped to collect a spotted shell the size and shape of a fir cone. 'Look at this,' he said, holding it up to Johnny.

A black, pointed hook, like a tiny sickle, was vainly stabbing at him from one end of the shell.

'Poisonous,' said Mick. 'If *that* gets you, you'll be very sick. You could even die.'

He put the shell back on the rocks while Johnny looked at it thoughtfully. Such a beautiful, innocent-looking object – yet it contained death! He did not forget that lesson in a hurry.

But he also learned that the reef was perfectly safe to explore if you followed two common-sense rules. The first was to watch where you were stepping; the second was never to touch anything unless you *knew* that it was harmless.

At last they reached the edge of the reef and stood looking down into the gently heaving sea. The tide was still going out, and water was pouring off the exposed coral down hundreds of little valleys it had carved in the living rock. There were large, deep pools here, open to the sea, and in them swam fish much bigger than any Johnny had seen before.

'Come along,' said Mick, adjusting his face mask. With scarcely a ripple, he slipped into the nearest pool, not even looking back to see if Johnny was following him.

Johnny hesitated for a moment, decided that he did not want to appear a coward, and lowered himself gingerly over the brittle coral. As soon as the water rose above his face mask, he forgot all his fears. The submarine world into which he had looked from above was even more beautiful, now that he was actually floating face down on the surface. He seemed like a fish himself, swimming in a giant aquarium, and able to see everything with crystal clarity through the window of his mask.

Very slowly, he followed Mick along the winding walls, be-tween coral cliffs that grew farther and farther apart as they approached the sea. At first the water was only two or three feet deep; then, quite abruptly, the bottom fell away almost vertically, and before Johnny realized what had happened, he was in water twenty feet deep. He had swum off the great plateau of the reef, and was heading for the open sea.

For a moment he was really frightened. He stopped swimming and marked time in the water, looking back over his shoulder to check that safety was only a few yards behind him. Then he looked ahead once more – ahead and downwards.

It was impossible to guess how far he could see into the depths – a hundred feet, at least. He was looking down a long, steep slope that led into a realm completely different from the brightly lit, colourful pools which he had just left. From a world sparkling with sunlight, he was staring into a blue, mysterious gloom. And far down in that gloom, huge shapes were moving back and forth in a stately dance.

'What are they?' he whispered to his companion.

'Groupers,' said Mick. 'Watch.' Then, to Johnny's alarm, he slipped beneath the surface and arrowed down into the depths, as swiftly and gracefully as any fish.

He became smaller and smaller as he approached those moving shapes, and they seemed to grow in size by comparison. When he stopped, perhaps fifty feet down, he was floating just above them. He reached out, trying to touch one of the huge fish, but it gave a flick of its tail and eluded him.

Mick seemed in no hurry to return to the surface, but Johnny had taken at least a dozen breaths while he was watching the performance. At last, to the great relief of his audience, Mick began to swim slowly upward, waving goodbye to the groupers as he did so.

'How big were those fish?' asked Johnny when Mick had popped out of the water and recovered his breath.

'Oh, only eighty, a hundred pounds. You should see the

really big ones up north. My grandfather hooked an eight-hundred-pounder off Cairns.'

'But you don't believe him,' grinned Johnny.

'But I do,' Mick grinned back. '*That* time he had a photograph to show it.'

As they swam back to the edge of the reef, Johnny glanced down once more into the blue depths, with their coral boulders, their overhanging terraces, and the ponderous shapes swimming slowly among them. It was a world as alien as another planet, even though it was here on his own Earth. And it was a world that, because it was so utterly strange, filled him with curiosity and with fear.

There was only one way of dealing with both these emotions. Sooner or later, he would have to follow Mick down that blue, mysterious slope.

Nine

'You're right, Professor,' said Dr Keith, 'though I'm darned if I know how you could tell. There's no large school of dolphins within the range of our hydrophones.'

'Then we'll go after them in the *Flying Fish.*'

'But where shall we look? They may be anywhere inside ten thousand square miles.'

'That's what the Survey Satellites are for,' Professor Kazan answered. 'Call Woomera Control and ask them to photograph an area of fifty miles radius around the island. Get them to do it as soon after dawn as possible. There must be a satellite going overhead some time tomorrow morning.'

'But why after dawn?' asked Keith. 'Oh, I see – the long shadows will make them easy to spot.'

'Of course. It will be quite a job searching such a huge area, and if we take too long over it, they'll be somewhere else.'

Johnny heard about the project soon after breakfast, when he was called in to help with the reconnaissance. It seemed that Professor Kazan had bitten off a little more than he could chew, for the island's picture-receiver had delivered twenty-five separate photographs, each covering an area of twenty miles on a side, and each showing an enormous amount of detail. They had been taken about an hour after dawn from a low-altitude meteorological satellite five hundred miles up, and since there were no clouds to obscure the view, they were of excellent quality. The powerful telescopic cameras had brought the Earth to within only five miles.

Johnny had been given the least important, but most interesting, photo in the mosaic to examine. This was the central one, showing the island itself. It was fascinating to go over it with a magnifying glass and to see the buildings and paths and boats leap up to meet the eye. Even individual people could be detected as small black spots.

For the first time, Johnny realized the full enormous extent of the reef around Dolphin Island. It stretched for miles away to the east, so that the island itself appeared merely like the point in a punctuation mark. Although the tide was in, every detail of the reef could be seen through the shallow water that covered it. Johnny almost forgot the job he was supposed to be doing as he explored the pools and submarine valleys and the hundreds of little canyons that had been worn by water draining off the reef shelf at low tide.

The searchers were in luck; the school was spotted sixty miles to the south-east of the island, almost on the extreme edge of the photo-mosaic. It was quite unmistakable: there were scores of dark bodies shooting along the surface, some of them frozen by the camera as they leaped clear of the sea. And one could tell from the widening Vs of their wakes that they were heading west.

Professor Kazan looked at the photograph with satisfaction. 'They're getting closer,' he said. 'If they've kept to that course, we can meet them in an hour. Is the *Flying Fish* ready?'

'She's still refuelling, but she can leave in thirty minutes.'

The Professor glanced at his watch; he seemed as excited as a small boy who had been promised a treat.

'Good,' he said briskly. 'Everyone at the jetty in twenty minutes.'

Johnny was there in five. It was the first time he had ever been aboard a boat (the *Santa Anna*, of course, hardly counted, for he had seen so little), and he was determined not to miss anything. He had already been ordered down from the cruiser's crow's-nest, thirty feet above the deck, when the Professor came aboard – smoking a huge cigar, wearing an eye-searing Hawaiian shirt, and carrying camera, binoculars, and briefcase. 'Let's go!' he said. The *Flying Fish* went.

She stopped again at the edge of the reef, when she had emerged from the channel cut through the coral.

'What're we waiting for?' Johnny asked Mick as they leaned over the handrails and looked at the receding island.

'I'm not sure,' Mick answered, 'but I can guess – ah, here they come! The Professor probably called them through the underwater speakers, though they usually turn up anyway.'

Two dolphins were approaching the *Flying Fish*, jumping high in the air as if to draw attention to themselves. They came right up to the boat – and, to Johnny's surprise, were promptly taken aboard. This was done by a crane which lowered a canvas sling into the water; as each of the dolphins swam into it in turn, it was raised on deck and dropped into a small tank of water at the stern. There was barely room for the two animals in this little aquarium, but they seemed perfectly at ease. Clearly, they had done this many times before.

'Einar and Peggy,' said Mick. 'Two of the brightest dolphins we ever had. The Professor let them loose several years ago, but they never go very far away.'

'How can you tell one from the other?' asked Johnny. 'They all look the same to me.'

Mick scratched his fuzzy head.

'Now you ask me, I'm not sure I can say. But Einar's easy – see that scar on his left flipper? And his girl friend is usually Peggy, so there you are. Well, I *think* it's Peggy,' he added doubtfully.

The *Flying Fish* had picked up speed, and was now moving away from the island at about ten knots. Her skipper (one of Mick's numerous uncles) was waiting until they were clear of all underwater obstacles before giving her full throttle.

The reef was two miles astern when he let down the big skis and opened up the hydro-jets. With a surge of power, the *Flying Fish* lurched forward, then slowly gained speed and rose out of the water. In a few hundred yards, the whole body of the boat was clear of the sea, and her drag had been reduced to a fraction of its normal amount. She could skate above the waves at fifty knots, with the same power that she needed to plough through them at ten.

It was exhilarating to stand on the open foredeck – keeping a firm grip of the rigging – and to face the gale that the boat made as she skimmed the ocean. But after a while, somewhat windswept and breathless, Johnny retreated to the sheltered space behind the bridge and watched Dolphin Island sink behind the horizon. Soon it was only a green-covered raft of white sand floating on the sea; then it was a narrow bar on the skyline; then it was gone.

They passed several similar, but smaller, islands in the next hour; they were all, according to Mick, quite uninhabited. From a distance they looked so delightful that Johnny wondered why they had been left empty in this crowded world. He had not been on Dolphin Island long enough to realize all the problems of power, water, and supplies that were involved if one wished to establish a home on the Great Barrier Reef.

There was no land in sight when the *Flying Fish* suddenly slowed down, plopped back into the water, and came to a dead halt.

'Quiet, please, everybody,' shouted the skipper. 'Prof wants to do some listening!'

He did not listen for long. After about five minutes, he emerged from the cabin, looking rather pleased with himself.

'We're on the right track,' he announced. 'They're within five miles of us, chattering at the tops of their voices.'

The *Flying Fish* set off again, a few points to the west of her original course. And in ten minutes she was surrounded by dolphins.

There were hundreds of them, making their easy, effortless way across the sea. When the *Flying Fish* came to rest, they crowded around her as if they had been expecting such a visit; perhaps, indeed, they had.

The crane was brought into action, and Einar was lowered over the side. But only Einar, for, as the Professor explained, 'There'll be a good many boisterous males down there, and we don't want any trouble while Einar's scouting around for us.' Peggy was indignant, but there was nothing she could do about it except splash everyone who came within range.

This, thought Johnny, must be one of the strangest conferences that has ever taken place. He stood with Mick on the fore-deck, leaning over the side and looking down at the sleek, dark-grey bodies gathered round Einar. What were they saying? Could Einar fully understand the language of his deep-sea cousins – and could the Professor understand Einar?

Whatever the outcome of this meeting, Johnny felt a deep gratitude towards these friendly, graceful creatures. He hoped that Professor Kazan could help them, as they had helped him.

After half an hour, Einar swam back into the sling and was hoisted aboard, to Peggy's great relief – as well as to the Professor's.

'I hope most of that was just gossip,' he remarked. 'Thirty minutes of solid Dolphin talk means a week's work, even with all the help the computer can give me.'

Below deck, the engines of the *Flying Fish* roared into life, and once again the ship lifted slowly out of the water. The dolphins kept up with it for a few hundred yards, but they were soon hopelessly outpaced. This was one speed contest in which they could not compete. The last that Johnny saw of them was a frieze of distant, dark bodies, leaping against the skyline, and already miles astern.

Ten

Johnny began his skin-diving lessons at the edge of the jetty, among the anchored fishing boats. The water was crystal clear, and as it was only four or five feet deep, he could make all his beginner's mistakes in perfect safety while he learned the use of flippers and face mask.

Mick was not a very good teacher. He had been able to swim and dive all his life, and could no longer remember his early troubles. To him it seemed incredible that *anyone* could fail to go effortlessly down to the sea-bed, or could not remain there in complete comfort for two or three minutes. So he grew quite impatient when his pupil remained bobbing about on the surface like a cork, with his legs kicking up in the air, unable to submerge more than a few inches.

Before long, however, Johnny got the right idea. He learned *not* to fill his lungs before a dive; that turned him into a balloon and gave him so much buoyancy that he simply couldn't go under. Next, he found that if he threw his legs clear out of the water, their unsupported weight drove him straight down. Then, once his feet were well below the surface, he could start kicking with his flippers, and they would drive him easily in any direction.

After a few hours of practice, he lost his initial clumsiness. He discovered the delights of swooping and gliding in a weightless world, like a spaceman in orbit. He could do loops and rolls, or hover motionless at any depth. But he could not stay under for even half as long as Mick; like everything that was worth doing, that would take time and practice.

He knew now that he had the time. Professor Kazan, although mild-mannered, was a person who wielded a great deal of influence, and he had seen to that. Wires had been pulled, forms had been filled in, and Johnny was now officially on the island establishment. His aunt had been only too eager to agree and had gladly forwarded the few belongings he valued. Now that he was on the other side of the world and could look back at his past life with more detachment, Johnny wondered if some of the fault might have been his. Had he really tried to fit into the household that had adopted him? He knew that his widowed aunt had not had an easy time. When he was older, he might understand her problems better, and perhaps they could be friends. But whatever happened, he did not for one moment regret that he had run away.

It was as if a new chapter had opened in his life – one that had no connection with anything that had gone before. He realized that until now he had merely existed; he had not really *lived*. Having lost those he loved while he was so young, he had been scared of making fresh attachments; worse than that, he had become suspicious and self-centred. But now he was changing, as the warm communal life of the island swept away the barriers of his reserve.

The fisherfolk were friendly, good-natured, and not too hard-working. There was no need for hard work, in a place where it was never cold and one had only to reach into the sea to draw out food. Every night, it seemed, there would be a dance or a movie show or a barbecue on the beach. And when it rained – as it sometimes did, at the rate of several inches an hour – there was always television. Thanks to the relay satellites, Dolphin Island was less than half a second from any city on Earth. The islanders could see everything that the rest of the world had to offer, while still being comfortably detached from it. They had most of the advantages of civilization and few of its defects.

But it was not all play for Johnny by any means. Like every other islander under twenty (and many of them over that age), he had to spend several hours a day at school.

Professor Kazan was keen on education, and the island had twelve teachers – two human, ten electronic. This was about the usual proportion, since the invention of teaching machines in the middle of the twentieth century had at last put education on a scientific basis.

All the machines were coupled to OSCAR, the big computer which did the Professor's translating, handled most of the island's administration and book-keeping, and could play championship chess on demand. Soon after Johnny's arrival, OSCAR had given him a thorough quiz to discover his level of education, then had prepared suitable instruction tapes and printed a training programme for him. Now he spent at least three hours a day at the keyboard of a teaching machine, typing out his responses to the information and questions flashed on the screen. He could choose his own time for his classes, but he knew better than to skip them. If he did so, OSCAR reported it at once to the Professor – or, worse still, to Dr Keith.

At the moment, the two scientists had much more important matters to bother about. After twenty-four hours of continuous work, Professor Kazan had translated the message that Einar had brought back – and it had placed him fairly and squarely on the horns of a dilemma. The Professor was a man of peace. If there was one phrase that summed him up, it was 'kind-hearted'. And now, to his great distress, he was being asked to take sides in a war.

He glared at the message that OSCAR had typed out, as if hoping that it would go away. But he had only himself to blame; after all, *he* was the one who had insisted on going after it.

'Well, Professor,' asked Dr Keith who, tired and unshaven, was slumped over the tape-control desk, 'now what are we going to do?'

'I haven't the faintest idea,' said Professor Kazan. Like most good scientists, and very few bad ones, he was never ashamed to admit when he was baffled. 'What would *you* suggest?'

'It seems to me that this is where our Advisory Committee would be useful. Why not talk it over with a couple of the members?'

'That's not a bad idea,' said the Professor. 'Let's see who we can contact at this time of day.' He pulled a list of names out of a drawer and started running his finger down the columns.

'Not the Americans – they'll all be sleeping. Ditto most of the Europeans. That leaves – let's see – Saha in Delhi, Hirsch in Tel Aviv, Abdullah in—'

'That's enough!' interrupted Dr Keith. 'I've never known a conference-call do anything useful with more than five people in it.'

'Right – we'll see if we can get these.'

A quarter of an hour later, five men scattered over half the globe were talking to each other as if they were all in the same room. Professor Kazan had not asked for vision, though that could have been provided, if necessary. Sound was quite sufficient for the exchange of views he wanted.

'Gentlemen,' he began, after the initial greetings, 'we have a problem. It will have to go to the whole Committee before long – and perhaps much higher than that – but I'd like your unofficial opinions first.'

'Ha!' said Dr Hassim Abdullah, the great Pakistani biochemist, from his laboratory in Karachi. 'You must have asked me for at least a dozen "unofficial opinions" by now, and I don't recall that you took the slightest notice of any of them.'

'This time I may,' answered the Professor. The solemnity in his tone warned his listeners that this was no ordinary discussion.

Quickly he outlined the events leading up to Johnny's arrival on the island. They were already familiar to his audience, for this strange rescue had received world-wide publicity. Then he described the sequel – the voyage of the *Flying Fish* and Einar's parley with the deep-sea dolphins.

'That may go down in the history books,' he said, 'as the first conference between Man and an alien species. I'm sure it won't be the last, so what we do now may help to shape the future – in space, as well as on Earth.

'Some of you, I know, think I've over-estimated the intelligence of dolphins. Well, now you can judge for yourselves. They've come to *us*, asking for help against the most ruthless of their enemies. There are only two creatures in the sea that normally attack them. The shark, of course, is one, but he's not a serious danger to a school of adult dolphins; they can kill him by ramming him in the gills. Because he's only a stupid fish – stupid even *for* a fish – they have nothing but contempt and hatred for him.

'The other enemy is a different matter altogether because he's their cousin, the killer whale, *Orcinus orca*. It's not far wrong to say that *orca* is a giant dolphin who's turned cannibal. He grows up to thirty feet in length, and specimens have been found with twenty dolphins in their stomachs. Think of that – an appetite that needs twenty dolphins at a time to satisfy it!

'No wonder that they've appealed to us for protection. They know that we've got powers they can't match – our ships have been proof of that for centuries. Perhaps, during all these ages, their friendliness to us has been an attempt to make contact, to ask for our help in their continual war – and only now have we had the intelligence to understand them. If that's true, I feel ashamed of myself – and my species.'

'Just a minute, Professor,' interrupted Dr Saha, the Indian physiologist. 'This is all very interesting, but are you *quite* certain that your interpretation is correct? Don't get upset, but we all know your affection for dolphins, which most of us share. Are you sure you haven't put your own ideas into their mouths?'

Some men might have been annoyed by this, even though Dr Saha had spoken as tactfully as possible. But Professor Kazan replied mildly enough.

'There's no doubt – ask Keith.'

'That's correct,' Dr Keith confirmed. 'I can't translate Dolphin as well as the Professor, but I'd stake my reputation on this.'

'Anyway,' continued Professor Kazan. 'My next point should prove that I'm not hopelessly pro-dolphin, however fond of them I happen to be. I'm not a zoologist, but I know something about the balance of nature. Even if we *could* help them, *should* we? Dr Hirsch, you may have some ideas on that.'

The Director of the Tel-Aviv Zoo took his time in answering; he was still a little sleepy, for it was not yet dawn in Israel.

'This is a hot potato you've handed us,' he grumbled. 'And I doubt if you've thought of all the complications. In the natural state, all animals have enemies – predators – and it would be disastrous for them if they didn't. Look at Africa, for example, where you've got lions and antelopes sharing the same territory. Suppose you shot all the lions – what would happen then? I'll tell you: the antelopes would multiply until they stripped all the food, and then they'd starve.

'Whatever the antelopes think about it, the lions are very good for them. Besides preventing them from outrunning their food supplies, they keep them fit, by eliminating the weaker specimens. That's Nature's way; it's cruel by our standards, but effective.'

'In this case the analogy breaks down,' said Professor Kazan. 'We're not dealing with wild animals but with intelligent people. They're not *human* people, but they're still people. So the correct analogy would be with a tribe of peaceable farmers who are continuously ravaged by cannibals. Would you say that the cannibals are good for the farmers – or would you try to reform the cannibals?'

Hirsch chuckled.

'Your point is well taken, though I'm not sure how you propose to reform killer whales.'

'Just a minute,' said Dr Abdullah. 'You're getting outside my territory. How bright *are* killer whales? Unless they really are as intelligent as dolphins, the analogy between human tribes breaks down, and there's no moral problem.'

'They're intelligent enough,' Professor Kazan answered unhappily. 'The few studies that have been made suggest that they're at least as intelligent as the other dolphins.'

'I suppose you know that famous story about the killers who tried to catch the Antarctic explorers?' said Dr Hirsch. The others admitted ignorance, so he continued: 'It happened back at the beginning of the last century, on one of the early expeditions to the South Pole – Scott's, I think. Anyway, a group of the explorers were on the edge of an ice-floe, watching some killer whales in the water. It never occurred to them that they were in any danger – until suddenly the ice beneath them started to shatter. The beasts were ramming it from underneath, and the men were lucky to jump to safety before they broke right through the ice. It was about three feet thick, too.'

'So they'll eat men if they have the chance,' said someone. 'You can count my vote against them.'

'Well, one theory was that they mistook the fur-clad explorers for penguins, but I'd hate to put it to the test. In any case, we're fairly sure that several skin-divers have been taken by them.'

There was a short silence while everyone digested this information. Then Dr Saha started the ball rolling again.

'Obviously, we need more facts before we come to any decisions. Someone will have to catch a few killer whales and make a careful study of them. Do you suppose you could make contact with them, Nickolai, as you have with dolphins?'

'Probably, though it might take years.'

'We're getting away from the point,' said Dr Hirsch impatiently. 'We've still got to decide *what* we should do, not *how* we do it. And I'm afraid there's another thundering big argument in favour of killer whales and against our dolphin friends.'

'I know what it is,' said Professor Kazan, 'but go ahead.'

'We get a substantial percentage of our food from the sea – about a hundred million tons of fish per annum. Dolphins are our direct competitors: what they eat is lost to us. You say there's a war between the killer whales and the dolphins, but there's also a war between dolphins and fishermen, who get their nets broken and their catches stolen. In *this* war, the killer whales are our allies. If they didn't keep the dolphin population under control, there might be no fish for us.'

Oddly enough, this did not seem to discourage the Professor. Indeed, he sounded positively pleased.

'Thank you, Mordecai – you've given me an idea. You know, of course, that dolphins have sometimes helped men to round up schools of fish, sharing the catch afterwards? It used to happen with the aborigines here in Queensland, two hundred years ago.'

'Yes, I know about that. Do you want to bring the custom up to date?'

'Among other ideas. Thank you very much, gentlemen; I'm extremely grateful to you. As soon as I've carried out a few experiments, I'll send a memorandum to the whole Committee and we'll have a full-scale meeting.'

'You might give us a few clues, after waking us up at this time in the morning.'

'Not yet, if you don't mind – until I know which ideas are utterly insane and which ones are merely crazy. Give me a couple of weeks, and meanwhile, you might inquire if anyone has a killer whale that I can borrow. Preferably one that won't eat more than a thousand pounds of food a day.'

Eleven

Johnny's first trip across the reef at night was an experience
he remembered all his life. The tide was out, there was no
Moon, and the stars were brilliant in a cloudless sky when he
and Mick set off from the beach, equipped with waterproof
flashlights, spears, face-masks, gloves, and sacks, which they
hoped to fill with crayfish. Many of the reef's inhabitants left
their hiding places only after dark, and Mick was particularly
anxious to find some rare and beautiful shells which never appeared in the daytime. He made a good deal of money selling
these to mainland collectors – quite illegally, as the island
fauna was supposed to be protected under the Queensland
Fisheries Act.

They crunched across the exposed coral, with their flashlights throwing pools of light ahead of them – pools that
seemed very tiny in the enormous darkness of the reef. The
night was so black that by the time they had gone a hundred
yards there was no sign of the island; luckily, a red warning
beacon on one of the radio masts served as a landmark. Without this to give them their bearings, they would have been hopelessly lost. Even the stars were not a safe guide, for they swung
across much of the sky in the time it took to reach the edge of
the reef and to return.

In any event, Johnny had to concentrate so hard on picking
a way across the brittle, shadowy coral world, that he had little
time to look at the stars. But when he did glance up, he was
struck by something so strange that for a moment he could only
stare at it in amazement.

Reaching up from the western horizon, almost to a point

overhead, was an enormous pyramid of light. It was faint but perfectly distinct; one might have mistaken it for the glow of a far-off city. Yet there were no cities for a hundred miles in that direction – only empty sea.

'What on earth is *that*?' asked Johnny at last. Mick, who had gone on ahead while he was staring at the sky, did not realize for a moment what was puzzling him.

'Oh,' he said, 'you can see it almost every clear night when there's no Moon. It's something out in space, I think. Can't you see it from your country?'

'I've never noticed it, but we don't have nights as clear as this.'

So the two boys stood gazing, flashlights extinguished for the moment, at a heavenly wonder that few men have seen since the glare and smoke of cities spread across the world and dimmed the splendour of the skies. It was the Zodiacal Light, which astronomers puzzled over for ages until they discovered that it was a vast halo of dust around the Sun.

Soon afterwards, Mick caught his first crayfish. It was crawling across the bottom of a shallow pool, and the poor creature was so confused by the electric glare that it could do nothing to escape. Into Mick's sack it went; and soon it had company. Johnny decided that this was not a very sporting way to catch crays, but he would not let that spoil his enjoyment when he ate them later.

There were many other hunters foraging over the reef, for the beams of the flashlights revealed thousands of small crabs. Usually they would scuttle away as Johnny and Mick approached, but sometimes they would stand their ground and wave threatening claws at the two approaching monsters. Johnny wondered if they were brave or merely stupid.

Beautifully marked cowries and cone shells were also prowling over the coral; it was hard to realize that to the yet smaller creatures of the reef, even these slow-moving molluscs were deadly beasts of prey. All the wonderful and lovely world beneath Johnny's feet was a battlefield; every instant, countless murders and ambushes and assassinations were taking place in the silence around him.

They were now nearing the edge of the reef and were splashing through water a few inches deep. It was full of phosphorescence, so that with every step, stars burst out beneath their feet. Even when they stood still, the slightest movement sent sparkles of light rippling across the surface. Yet when they examined the water with the beams of their flashlights, it appeared to be completely empty. The creatures producing this display of luminescence were too tiny, or too transparent, to be seen.

Now the water was deepening, and in the darkness ahead of him, Johnny could hear the roar and thunder of waves beating against the edge of the reef. He moved slowly and cautiously, for though he must have been over this ground a dozen times by day, it seemed completely strange and unfamiliar in the narrow beams of the flashlights. He knew, however, that at any moment he might stumble into some deep pool or flooded valley.

Even so, he was taken by surprise when the coral suddenly fell away beneath his feet and he found himself standing at the very brink of a dark, mysterious pool. The beam of the torch seemed to penetrate only a few inches; though the water was crystal clear, the light was quickly lost in its depths.

'Sure to find some crays here,' said Mick. He lowered himself into the pool with scarcely a splash, leaving Johnny standing above, half a mile from land, in the booming darkness of the reef.

There was no need for him to follow; if he wished, he could remain here until Mick had finished. The pool looked very sinister and uninviting, and it was easy to imagine all sorts of monsters lurking in its depths.

But this was ridiculous, Johnny told himself. He had probably dived in this very pool and had already met all its inhabitants. They would be much more scared of him than he would be of them.

He inspected his flashlight carefully and lowered it into the water to check that it continued shining when submerged. Then he adjusted his face-mask, took half a dozen fast, deep breaths, and followed Mick.

The light from the torch was surprisingly powerful, now that both he and it were on the same side of the water barrier. But it revealed only the small patch of coral or sand upon which it fell; outside its narrow cone, everything was blackness – mystery – menace. In these initial seconds of Johnny's first night dive, panic was not far away. He had an almost irresistible impulse to look over his shoulder to see if anything was following him . . .

After a few minutes, however, he got control of his nerves. The sight of Mick's exploring beam of light, flashing and flickering through the submarine darkness a few yards away, reminded him that he was not alone. He began to enjoy peeping into caves and under ledges and coming face to face with startled fish. Once he met a beautifully patterned moray eel that snapped at him angrily from its hole in the rocks and waved its snake-like body in the water. Johnny did not care for those pointed teeth, but he knew that morays never attacked unless they were molested – and he had no intention of making enemies on this dive.

The pool was full of strange noises, as well as strange creatures. Every time Mick banged his spear against a rock, Johnny could hear the sound more loudly than if he had been in air. He could also hear – and sometimes feel through the water –

the thudding of the waves against the edge of the reef only a few yards away.

Suddenly he became aware of the new sound, like the patter of tiny hailstones. It was faint, but very clear, and seemed to come from close at hand. At the same moment, he noticed that the beam of his flashlight was beginning to fill with swirling fog.

Millions of little creatures, most of them no larger than grains of sand, had been attracted by the light and were hurling themselves against the lens, like moths into a candle. Soon they were coming in such countless numbers that the beam was completely blocked; those that missed the flashlight made Johnny's exposed skin tingle as they battered against him. They were moving at such a speed that he could not be certain of their shapes, though he thought that some of them looked rather like tiny shrimps about the size of rice grains.

These creatures, Johnny knew, must be the larger and more active of the plankton animals, the basic food of almost all the fish in the sea. He was forced to switch off his light until they had dispersed and he could no longer hear – or feel – the patter of their myriad bodies. As he waited for the living fog to drift away, he wondered if any larger creatures might be attracted by his light – sharks, for example. He was quite prepared to face them in the daytime, but it was a very different matter after sunset . . .

When Mick started to climb out of the pool, he was glad to follow. Yet he would not have missed this experience for anything; it had shown him another of the sea's many faces. Night could transform the world below the waves, as it transformed the world above. No one knew the sea who explored it only by daylight.

Indeed, only a small part of the sea ever knew daylight. Most of it was a realm of eternal darkness, for the rays of the sun could reach only a few hundred feet into its depths before being utterly absorbed. No light ever shone in the abyss – except the cold luminescence of the nightmare creatures who lived there, in a world without sun or seasons.

'What have you caught?' Johnny asked Mick when they had both clambered out of the pool.

'Six crayfish, two tiger cowries, three spider shells, and a volute I've never seen before. Not a bad haul – though there was a big cray I couldn't reach. I could see his feelers, but he backed into a cave.'

They started to walk homewards across the great plateau of living coral, using the beacon on the radio mast as their guide. That bright red star seemed miles away in the darkness, and Johnny was uncomfortably aware that the water through which he was wading had become much deeper while they had been exploring the pool. The tide was returning; it would be very unpleasant to be caught here, so far from land, while the sea went pouring in ahead of them.

But there was no danger of that; Mick had planned the excursion carefully. He had also, quite deliberately, used it to test his new friend, and Johnny had passed with flying colours.

There were some people whose nerves would never allow them to dive at night, when they could see only the tiny oval of a flashlight beam and could imagine anything in the remaining darkness. Johnny must have felt scared, as everyone did for the first time, but he had conquered his fears.

Soon he would be ready to leave these safe and sheltered pools and to do some *real* diving off the edge of the reef, in the ever-changing, unpredictable waters of the open sea.

Twelve

It was two weeks before anyone on the island saw the first of the Professor's ideas in action. There were, of course, many rumours, for as soon as the details of the dolphins' request were released, everyone had his own theories about what should be done.

The scientists of the research station were, as might be expected, actively pro-dolphin. Dr Keith summed up their views when he remarked, 'Even if killer whales do turn out to be the more intelligent of the two, I'll back the dolphins. They're much nicer people, and you don't choose your friends for their brains.' When Johnny heard this, he was quite surprised, as he still did not care for Dr Keith's patronizing attitude and regarded him as a cold fish with few human emotions. However, he must have *some* good qualities for Professor Kazan to have made him his assistant; by this time, anything that the Professor did was, as far as Johnny was concerned, beyond criticism.

The fishermen were divided. They, too, liked dolphins, but recognized them as competitors, for they knew at first-hand the arguments that Dr Hirsch had put forward. There were times when dolphins had torn holes in their nets, stolen most of their catch, and made them say things about his friends that Professor Kazan would have been very unhappy to hear. If killer whales kept the dolphin population from getting too large, then good luck to them.

Johnny listened to these discussions with interest, but he had already made up his mind; no mere facts were going to make him change it. When someone has saved your life, that settles the matter; nothing that anyone else can say will turn you against him.

By this time, Johnny had become quite a skilful diver, though he knew that he would never be as good as Mick. He had mastered the use of flippers, face-mask, and snorkel, and could now stay underwater for periods that would have astonished him only a few weeks ago. Though the healthy, open-air life was making him bigger and stronger, this was only part of the story. The first times he had dived he had been nervous, but now he felt as much at home undersea as on the land. He had learned to move smoothly and effortlessly through the water, and so could make a single lungful of air last much longer than when he had started his lessons. Whenever he felt like it, he could stay underwater for a full minute without straining himself.

He was doing all this for fun, and because diving was a skill worth acquiring for its own sake. Not until Professor Kazan called for him one afternoon did he learn how quickly his hobby would be of use.

The Professor looked tired but cheerful, as if he had been working night and day on some project that was going well. 'Johnny,' he said, 'I've a job for you, which I'm sure you'll enjoy. Take a look at this.'

The piece of apparatus he pushed across his desk was something like a very small adding machine, with twenty-five buttons arranged in five rows of five each. It was only about three inches square, with a curved, sponge-rubber base, and was fitted with straps and buckles. Obviously, it was intended to be worn on the forearm, like an overgrown wrist watch.

Some studs were blank, but most of them carried a single word engraved in large, clear letters. As he ran his eye across the face of the little keyboard, Johnny began to understand the purpose of the device.

The words he read were: NO, YES, UP, DOWN, FRIEND, RIGHT, LEFT, FAST, SLOW, STOP, GO, FOLLOW, COME, DANGER!

and HELP! They were arranged logically over the face of the keyboard: thus UP and DOWN were at top and bottom respectively; LEFT and RIGHT actually on the left and right. Opposing words like NO and YES or STOP and GO were as far apart as possible so that the wrong stud could not be pressed by mistake. The studs marked DANGER! and HELP! were covered by guards that had to be slipped aside before they could be operated.

'There's a lot of neat solid-state electronics inside that,' explained the Professor, 'and a battery good for fifty hours' operation. When you press one of those buttons, you won't hear anything except a faint buzz. A dolphin, however, will hear the word which is printed on the button, but in its own language – at least, we hope it will. What happens then is what we want to find out.

'If you're wondering about the blank studs, we've kept them until we decide what other words we need. Now, I want you to take this gadget – we'll call it a Mark I Communicator – and practise swimming and diving with it until it seems part of you. Get to know which stud is which, until you can find the one you want with your eyes shut. Then come back here, and we'll move on to the next experiment.'

Johnny was so excited that he sat up most of the night pressing buttons and memorizing the layout of the keyboard. When he presented himself to the Professor immediately after breakfast, the scientist looked pleased but not surprised.

'Get your flippers and face-mask,' he said, 'and meet me at the pool.'

'Can I bring Mick?' asked Johnny.

'Of course, as long as he keeps quiet and doesn't make a nuisance of himself.'

Mick was intrigued by the communicator, but not too happy that it had been entrusted to Johnny.

'I don't see why he's given it to *you* to try out,' he said.

'That's obvious,' Johnny answered very smugly. 'Dolphins like me.'

'Then they're not as intelligent as the Professor thinks,' retorted Mick. Normally, this would have started a quarrel, though not a fight, for the simple reason that Mick was almost twice as heavy as Johnny and more than twice as strong.

By a coincidence that was not particularly odd, Professor Kazan and Dr Keith were discussing the same problem as they walked down to the pool, heavily laden with equipment.

'Sputnik's behaviour towards Johnny,' said the Professor, 'is right in line with the cases in the history books. When a wild dolphin makes friends with a human being, it's almost always with a child.'

'And Johnny's exceptionally small for his age,' added Dr Keith. 'I suppose they feel happier with children than with adults because grown-ups are big and possibly dangerous. A child, on the other hand, is just about the same size as a young dolphin.'

'Exactly,' said the Professor. 'And the dolphins who make friends with bathers at seaside resorts are probably females who've lost their young. A human child may be a kind of substitute.'

'Here comes our Dolphin-boy,' said Dr Keith, 'looking very pleased with himself.'

'Which is more than one can say for Mick. I'm afraid I've hurt his feelings. But Sputnik's definitely scared of him. I let him go swimming in the pool once, and even Susie wasn't happy. You can keep him busy, helping you with the movie camera.'

A moment later the boys had caught up with the scientists, and Professor Kazan gave them his instructions. 'I want complete silence when we're at the pool,' he said. 'Any talking may ruin the experiment. Dr Keith and Mick will set up the camera on the east side, with the sun behind them. I'll go to the other side while you get into the water and swim to the middle. I expect Susie and Sputnik will follow you, but whatever happens, stay there until I wave you to go somewhere else. Understand?'

'Yes sir,' answered Johnny, very proud of himself.

The Professor was carrying a stack of large white cards, bearing the same words as the studs on the communicator.

'I'll hold up each of these in turn,' he said. 'When I do so, you press the right button – and make sure it *is* the right button. If I hold up two cards at once, press the button for the *top* card first, then the button for the lower one immediately afterwards. Is that clear?'

Johnny nodded.

'At the very end, I want to try something drastic. We'll give the DANGER! signal first, then the HELP! one a few seconds later. When you press that, I want you to splash around as if you're drowning, and sink slowly to the bottom. Now, repeat all that to me.'

When Johnny had finished doing this, they had reached the wire-net fence around the pool, and all conversation ceased. But there was still plenty of noise, for Susie and Sputnik welcomed them with loud squeaks and splashings.

Professor Kazan gave Susie her usual titbit, but Sputnik kept his distance and refused to be tempted. Then Johnny slipped into the water and swam slowly to the centre of the pool.

The two dolphins followed, keeping about twenty feet away. When Johnny looked back, with his head below the surface, he was able to appreciate for the first time the graceful way in which their rubbery bodies flexed up and down as their flukes propelled them through the water.

He floated in mid-pool, one eye on the Professor, the other on the dolphins, waiting for the cards to go up. The first was FRIEND.

There was no doubt that the dolphins heard that, for they became quite excited. Even to Johnny's ears, the buzzing of the communicator was clear enough, though he knew that he could hear only the low-frequency sounds that it was making, not the ultrasonic noise that conveyed most of the meaning to the dolphins.

FRIEND went up again, and again Johnny pressed the button. This time, to his delight, both dolphins started to move towards him. They swam to within only five feet and remained there, looking at him with their dark, intelligent eyes. He had the distinct impression that they had already guessed the purpose of this experiment, and were waiting for the next signal.

That was the word LEFT, which produced a wholly un-expected result. Susie immediately swung to her left, Sputnik turned to his *right*, and Professor Kazan started calling himself 'idiot' in each of the fourteen languages he spoke fluently. He had just realized that if you give an order, you should make sure that it has only one interpretation. Sputnik had assumed that Johnny meant his own left; the more self-centred Susie had assumed that he meant her left.

There was no ambiguity about the next order – DOWN. With a flurry of flukes, the dolphins dived to the bottom of the pool. They remained there patiently until Johnny gave the signal UP. He wondered how long they would have stayed there if he hadn't given it.

It was obvious that they were enjoying this new and wonder-ful game. Dolphins are the most playful of all animals, and will invent their own games even if none are shown to them. And perhaps Susie and Sputnik already realized that this was more than fun – it was the beginning of a partnership that might benefit both races.

The first pair of cards went up – GO FAST. Johnny pressed the two buttons one after the other. The second buzz had scarcely ceased to sound in his ears before both Susie and Sputnik were racing across the pool. While they were still travelling at high speed, they obeyed RIGHT and LEFT (*their* rights and lefts this time), checked for SLOW, and came to a halt for STOP.

The Professor was wild with delight, and even the unemotional Dr Keith was grinning all over his face as he recorded the scene, while Mick was leaping about the edge of the pool like one of his ancestors at a tribal dance. But suddenly everyone became solemn: the DANGER! card went up.

What would Susie and Sputnik do now? wondered Johnny as he pressed the button.

They just laughed at him. They knew that it was a game, and they weren't fooled. Their reactions were far quicker than his; they were familiar with every inch of the pool, and if there had really been danger here, they would have spotted it long before any sluggish human intelligence could have warned them.

Then Professor Kazan made a slight tactical error. He told Johnny to cancel the previous message by signalling NO DANGER.

At once the two dolphins flew into frantic, panic-stricken activity. They tore around the pool, leaped a good six feet in the air, and charged past Johnny at such speed and at such close quarters that he was scared they would accidentally ram him. This performance lasted for several minutes; then Susie stuck her head out of the water and made a very rude noise at the Professor. Not until then did the watchers realize that the dolphins had been having some fun at their expense.

There was still one signal to test. Would they take this as joke or treat it seriously? Professor Kazan waved the HELP! sign, Johnny pressed the button and went down, blowing an impressive stream of bubbles.

Two grey meteors raced through the water towards him. He felt a firm but gentle nudge, pushing him back to the surface. Even had he wished to, he could not have stayed under; the dolphins were holding him with his head above the water, just as they had been known to support their own companions when they were injured. Whether that HELP! was genuine or not, they were taking no chances.

The Professor was waving for him to return, and he began to swim back to shore. But now the dolphins' own exuberance had infected him. Out of sheer high spirits, he dived down to the bottom of the pool, looped-the-loop in the water, and swam on his back, facing up at the surface. He even imitated the animals' own movements, by keeping his legs and flippers together and trying to undulate through the water as they did. Although he made some progress, it was at about a tenth of their speed.

They followed him all the way back, sometimes brushing affectionately against him. As far as Susie and Sputnik were concerned, he knew that he need never press the FRIEND button again.

When he climbed out of the pool, Professor Kazan embraced him like a long-lost son; even Dr Keith, to Johnny's embarrassment, tried to clutch him with bony arms, and he had to side-step smartly to avoid him. As soon as they had left the silence zone, the two scientists started chattering like excited schoolboys.

'It's too good to be true,' said Dr Keith. 'Why, they were one jump ahead of us most of the time!'

'I noticed that,' answered the Professor. 'I'm not sure

whether they're better thinkers than we are, but they're certainly faster ones.'

'Can I use that gadget next time, Professor?' asked Mick plaintively.

'Yes,' said Professor Kazan at once. 'Now we know that they'll co-operate with Johnny, we want to see if they'll do so with other people. I picture trained diver-dolphin teams that can open up new frontiers in the sea for research, salvage – oh, a thousand jobs.' He suddenly stopped, in the full flight of his enthusiasm. 'I've just remembered two words that should have gone into the communicator; we must put them there at once.'

'What are they?' asked Dr Keith.

'PLEASE and THANK YOU,' answered the Professor.

Thirteen

For more than a hundred years, Dolphin Island had been haunted by a legend. Johnny would have heard of it soon enough, but, as it happened, he made the discovery by himself.

He had been taking a short-cut through the forest, which covered three-quarters of the island, and, as usual, it turned out to be not short at all. Almost as soon as he left the path, he lost his direction in the densely packed pandanus and pisonia trees, and was floundering up to his knees in the sandy soil that the muttonbirds had riddled with their burrows.

It was a strange feeling, being 'lost' only a few hundred feet from the crowded settlement and all his friends. He could easily imagine that he was in the heart of some vast jungle, a thousand miles from civilization. There was all the loneliness and mystery of the untamed wild, with none of its danger, for if he pushed on in any direction, he would be out of the tiny forest in five minutes. True, he wouldn't come out in the place he had intended, but that hardly mattered on so small an island.

Suddenly he became aware of something odd about the patch of jungle into which he had blundered. The trees were smaller and farther apart than elsewhere, and as he looked around him, Johnny slowly realized that this had once been a clearing in the forest. It must have been abandoned a long, long time ago, for it had become almost completely overgrown. In a few more years, all trace of it would be lost.

Who could have lived here, he wondered, years before radio and aircraft had brought the Great Barrier Reef into contact with the world? Criminals? Pirates? All sorts of romantic ideas flashed through his mind, and he began to poke around among the roots of the trees to see what he could find.

He had become a little discouraged, and was wondering if he was simply imagining things, when he came across some smoke-blackened stones, half-covered by leaves and earth. A fireplace, he decided, and redoubled his efforts. Almost at once, he found some pieces of rusty iron, a cup that had lost its handle, and a broken spoon.

That was all. It was not a very exciting treasure trove, but it did prove that civilized people, not savages, had been here long ago. No one would come to Dolphin Island, so far from land, merely to have a picnic; whoever they were, they must have had a good reason.

Taking the spoon as a souvenir, Johnny left the clearing, and ten minutes later was back on the beach. He went in search of Mick, whom he found in the class-room, nearing the end of

Mathematics II, tape 3. As soon as Mick had finished, switched off the teaching machine, and thumbed his nose at it, Johnny showed him the spoon and described where he had found it.

To his surprise, Mick seemed ill-at-ease.

'I wish you hadn't taken that,' he said. 'Better put it back.'

'But why?' asked Johnny in amazement.

Mick was quite embarrassed. He scuffed his large, bare feet on the polished plastic floor and did not answer directly.

'Of course,' he said, 'I don't *really* believe in ghosts, but I'd hate to be there by myself on a dark night.'

Johnny was now getting a little exasperated, but he knew that he'd have to let Mick tell the story in his own way. Mick began by taking Johnny to the Message Centre, putting through a local call to the Brisbane Museum, and speaking a few words to the Assistant Curator of the Queensland History Department.

A few seconds later, a strange object appeared on the vision screen. It was a small iron tank, or cistern, about four feet square and two feet deep, standing in a glass display case. Beside it were two crude oars.

'What do you think *that* is?' asked Mick.

'It looks like a water tank to me,' said Johnny.

'Yes,' said Mick, 'but it was a boat, too, and it sailed from this island a hundred and thirty years ago – with three people in it.'

'*Three* people – in a thing that size!'

'Well, one was a baby. The grownups were an English-woman, Mary Watson, and her Chinese cook, whose name I don't remember – it was Ah Something...'

As the strange story unfolded, Johnny was transported back in time to an age that he could scarcely imagine. Yet it was only 1881 – not yet a century and a-half ago. There had been telephones and steam engines then, and Albert Einstein had already been born. But along the Great Barrier Reef, cannibals still paddled their war canoes.

Despite this, the young husband, Captain Watson had set up his home on Dolphin Island. His business was collecting and selling sea cucumbers, or *bêche-de-mer*, the ugly, sausage-like creatures that crawled sluggishly in every coral pool. The Chinese paid high prices for the dried skins, which they valued for medical purposes.

Soon the island's supplies of *bêche-de-mer* were exhausted, and the Captain had to search farther and farther from home. He was away in his small ship for weeks at a time, leaving his young wife to look after the house and their new-born son, with the help of two Chinese servants.

It was while the Captain was away that the savages landed. They killed one of the Chinese houseboys and seriously injured the other, before Mary Watson drove them off with rifle and revolver. But she knew that they would return – and that her husband's ship would not be back for another month.

The situation was desperate, but Mary Watson was a brave and resourceful woman. She decided to escape from the island, with the baby and the houseboy, in a small iron tank used for boiling *bêche-de-mer*, hoping to be picked up by one of the ships plying along the Reef.

She stocked her tiny, unstable craft with food and water, and paddled away from her home. The houseboy was gravely injured and could give her little help, and her four-month-old son must have needed constant attention. She had just one stroke of luck, without which the voyage would not have lasted ten minutes: the sea was perfectly calm.

The next day they grounded on a neighbouring reef and remained there for two days, hoping to see a boat. But no ships came in sight, so they pushed off again and eventually reached a small island, forty-two miles from their starting point.

And it was from this island that they saw a steamer going by, but no one on board noticed Mrs Watson frantically waving her baby's shawl.

Now they had exhausted all their water, and there was none on the island. Yet they survived another four days, slowly dying of thirst, hoping for rains that never came and for ships that never appeared.

Three months later, quite by chance, a passing schooner sent men ashore to search for food. Instead, they found the body of the Chinese cook, and, hidden in the undergrowth, the iron tank. Huddled inside it was Mary Watson, with her baby son still in her arms. And beside her was the log of the eight-day voyage, which she had kept to the very end.

'I've seen it in the Museum,' said Mick, very solemnly. 'It's on half a dozen sheets of paper, torn out of a notebook. You can still read most of it, and I'll never forget the last entry. It just says: "No water – nearly dead with thirst."'

For a long time, neither boy said anything. Then Johnny looked at the broken spoon he was still holding. It was foolish, of course, but he *would* put it back, out of respect for Mary Watson's gallant ghost. He could understand the feelings of Mick and his people towards her memory. He wondered how often, on moonlit nights, the more imaginative islanders did believe that they had seen a young woman pushing an iron box out to sea . . .

Then another, and much more disturbing, thought suddenly struck him. He turned towards Mick, wondering just how to put the question. But it was not necessary, for Mick answered without prompting.

'I feel pretty bad about the whole thing,' he said, 'even though it was such a long time ago. You see, I know for a fact that my grandfather's grandfather helped to eat the other Chinaman.'

Fourteen

Every day now, Johnny and Mick would go swimming with the two dolphins, trying to find the limits of their intelligence and their co-operation. They now tolerated Mick and would obey his requests when he was using the communicator, but they remained unfriendly to him. Sometimes they would try to scare him, by charging him with teeth showing, then turning aside at the last possible moment. They never played such tricks with Johnny, though they would often nibble at his flippers or rub gently against him, expecting to be tickled and stroked in return.

This prejudice upset Mick, who couldn't see why Susie and Sputnik preferred, as he put it, 'an undersized little pale-skin' like Johnny. But dolphins are as temperamental as human people, and there is no accounting for tastes. Mick's opportunity was to come later, though in a way that no one could have guessed.

Despite occasional arguments and quarrels, the boys were now firm friends and were seldom far apart. Mick was, indeed, the first really close friend that Johnny had ever made. There was good reason for this, though he did not know it. After losing both his parents, at such early age, he had been afraid to risk his affections elsewhere, but now the break with his past was so complete that it had lost much of its power over him.

Besides, Mick was someone whom anybody could admire. Like most of the islanders, he had a splendid physique; generations of sea-battling forefathers had made sure of that. He was alert and intelligent and full of information about things of which Johnny had never heard. His faults were minor ones – rashness, exaggeration, and a fondness for practical jokes, which sometimes got him into trouble.

Towards Johnny he felt protective, almost fatherly, as a big man can often be towards a much smaller one. And perhaps the warm-hearted island boy, with four brothers, three sisters, and scores of aunts, uncles, cousins, nephews, and nieces, felt the inner loneliness of this runaway orphan from the other side of the world.

Ever since he had mastered the basic technique of diving, Johnny had been pestering Mick to take him exploring off the edge of the reef, where he could test his new skills in deep water and among big fish. But Mick had taken his time. Though he was impatient in small matters, he could be cautious in big ones. He knew that diving in a small, safe pool, or close to the jetty, was very different from operating in the open sea. So many things could go wrong: there were powerful currents, unexpected storms might spring up, sharks might make a nuisance of themselves – the sea was full of surprises, even for the most experienced diver. It was merciless to those who made mistakes and did not give them a second chance.

Johnny's opportunity came in a way that he had not expected. Susie and Sputnik were responsible. Professor Kazan had decided that it was time they went out into the world to earn their own living. He never kept a pair of dolphins longer than a year, believing that it was not fair to do so. They were social creatures and needed to make contact with their own kind. Most of his subjects, when he released them, remained close to the island and could always be called through the underwater loud-speakers. He was quite sure that Susie and Sputnik would behave in the same way.

In fact, they simply refused to leave. When the gate of the pool was opened, they swam a little way down the channel leading into the sea, then darted back as if afraid that they would be shut outside.

'I know what's wrong,' said Mick in disgust. 'They're so used to being fed by us that they're too lazy to catch their own fish.'

There might have been some truth in that, but it was not the the whole explanation. For when Professor Kazan asked Johnny to swim down the channel, they followed him out to sea. He did not even have to press any of the buttons on the communicator.

After that, there was no more swimming in the deserted pool, for which, though no one knew it, Professor Kazan now had other purposes in mind. Every morning, immediately after their first session at school, Mick and Johnny would meet the two dolphins and head out to the reef. Usually they took Mick's surf-board with them, as a floating base on which they could load their gear and any fish that they caught.

Mick told a hair-raising tale of sitting on this same board while a tiger shark prowled around, trying to take a bite out of a thirty-pound barracuda he'd shot and foolishly left dangling in the water. 'If you want to live a long time on the Great Barrier Reef,' he said, 'get your speared fish out of the sea as quickly as you can. Australian sharks are the meanest in the world – they grab three or four divers every year.'

That was nice to know; Johnny wondered how long it would take a shark to chew through the two inches of foam-and-fibreglass in Mick's board, if it really tried . . .

But with Susie and Sputnik as escorts, there was no danger from sharks; indeed, they hardly ever saw one. The presence of the two dolphins gave them a wonderful sense of security, such as no diver in the open sea could ever have felt before. Sometimes Susie and Sputnik were joined by Einar and Peggy, and once a school of at least fifty dolphins accompanied them on one of their swims. This was too much of a good thing, for the water was so crowded that visibility was almost zero; but Johnny could not bring himself to hurt their feelings by pressing the GO button.

He had swum often enough in the shallow pools on the great coral plateau around the island, but to dive off the reef's outer edge was a much more awe-inspiring experience. The water was sometimes so clear that Johnny felt he was floating in mid-air, with no means of support. He could look down and see absolutely nothing between himself and a jagged coral landscape forty feet below, and he had to keep reminding himself that it was impossible to fall.

In some areas the great fringing reef around the island ended sharply in an almost vertical wall of coral. It was fascinating to sink slowly down the face of this wall, surprising the gorgeously coloured fish that lived in its cracks and recesses. At the end of a dive, Johnny would try to identify the most striking of the reef butterflies in the Institute's reference books, but he usually found that they had no popular names, only unpronounceable Latin ones.

Almost everywhere one might run into isolated boulders and pinnacles, rising suddenly out of the sea-bed and reaching almost to the surface. Mick called these 'bommies', and sometimes they reminded Johnny of the carved rock formations in the Grand Canyon. These, however, had not been shaped by the forces of erosion; they had *grown* into their present forms, for they were the accumulated skeletons of countless coral animals. Only the thin surface was now alive, over a massive core of dead limestone weighing many tons, and ten or twenty feet high. When the underwater visibility was poor, as was sometimes the case after a storm or rain shower, it was startling to come across one of these stone monsters looming suddenly out of the mist.

Many of them were riddled with caves, and these caves were

always inhabited; it was not a good idea to enter them until you had discovered who was at home. It might be a moray eel, constantly snapping his hideous jaws; it might be a family of friendly but dangerous scorpion fish, waving their poison-tipped spines like a bundle of turkey feathers; and if the cave was a large one, it would usually be a rock-cod, or grouper. Some of these were much bigger than Johnny, but they were quite harmless and backed nervously away when he approached them.

In a surprisingly short time he grew to recognize individual fish and to know where to find them. The groupers never strayed far from their own particular caves, and Johnny soon began to look on some of them as personal friends. One scarred veteran had a fish-hook embedded in his lower lip, with a piece of line still hanging from it. Despite his unfortunate experience with mankind, he was not unfriendly and even allowed Johnny to come close enough to stroke him.

The groupers, the morays, the scorpion fish – these were the permanent residents of the submarine landscape that Johnny was beginning to know and love. But sometimes there would be unexpected and exciting visitors swimming in from deeper water. It was part of the reef's attraction that you never knew what you would meet on any given dive, even in an area that you had visited a dozen times before and knew like the proverbial back of your hand.

Sharks were, of course, the commonest prowlers of the reef. Johnny never forgot the first he met, one day when he and Mick had given their escorts the slip by going out an hour earlier than usual. He never saw it coming; it was suddenly there, a grey, superbly streamlined torpedo, moving slowly and effortlessly towards him. It was so beautiful and so graceful that it was impossible to think of it as dangerous. Not until it had approached to within twenty feet did Johnny look around anxiously for Mick. He was relieved to find his friend snorkling immediately above him, eyeing the situation calmly but with loaded spear gun at the ready.

The shark, like almost all sharks, was merely inquisitive. It looked Johnny over with its cold, staring eyes – so different from the friendly, intelligent eyes of the dolphins – and swerved off to the right when it was ten feet away. Johnny had a perfect view of the pilot fish swimming in front of its nose, and the remora, or sucker fish, clamped onto its back – an ocean-going hitch-hiker, using his suction pad to give him a free ride through life.

There was nothing that a diver could do about sharks, except to watch out for them and to leave them alone, in the hope that they would do the same to him. If you faced up to them, they would always go away. But if you lost your nerve and tried to run – well, anyone who was stupid enough to run deserved little sympathy, for a shark could swim thirty miles per hour to a skin-diver's three, without even exerting himself.

More unnerving than any sharks were the packs of barracuda that roamed along the edge of the reef. Johnny was very glad that the surf-board was floating overhead the first time he discovered that the water around him was full of the silver sea pike, with their hostile eyes and aggressive, under-slung jaws. They were not very large – three feet long at the most – but there were hundreds of them, and they formed a circular wall, with Johnny at the centre. It was a wall that came closer and closer as the barracuda spiralled in to get a better look at him, until presently he could see nothing but their glittering bodies. Though he waved his arms and shouted into the water, it made not the slightest difference: they inspected him at their leisure – then, for no reason that he could see, turned suddenly away and disappeared into the blue.

Johnny surfaced, grabbed the board, and held an anxious

conference with Mick across it. Every few seconds he kept bobbing his head underwater, to see if the wolf pack had returned.

'They won't bother you,' said Mick reassuringly. ''Cuda are cowards. If you shoot one, all the others will run away.'

Johnny was glad to know it and took the next meeting more calmly. All the same, he never felt quite happy when the silver hunters closed in on him, like a fleet of spaceships from an alien world. Perhaps some day, one of them would risk a nibble, and then the whole pack would move in . . .

There was one serious difficulty about exploring the reef: it was *too* big. Most of it was far beyond comfortable swimming range, and there were areas out towards the horizon that had never been visited. Often Johnny wished he could have gone farther into unknown territory, but he had been forced to save his strength for the long swim home. It was on one of these weary return journeys, as he helped Mick to push the surfboard loaded with at least a hundred pounds of fish, that the answer occurred to him.

Mick was sceptical, but agreed that the idea would be splendid – if it worked. 'It's not going to be easy,' he said, 'to make a harness that will fit a dolphin. They're so streamlined that it will slide off them.'

'I'm thinking of a kind of elastic collar, just ahead of the flippers. If it's broad enough and tight enough, it should stay on. Let's not talk about it, though – people will only laugh at us.'

This was good advice, but impossible to carry out. Everyone wanted to know *why* they needed sponge rubber, elastic webbing, nylon cord, and oddly shaped pieces of plastic, and they had to confess the truth. There was no hope of carrying out the first trials in secrecy, and Johnny had an embarrassingly large audience when he fitted his harness on Susie.

He ignored the jokes and suggestions from the crowd as he buckled the straps around the dolphin. She was so trusting that she made no objection, being quite confident that Johnny would do nothing to harm her. This was a strange new game, and she was willing to learn the rules.

The harness fitted over the front part of the dolphin's tapering body, being prevented from slipping back (so Johnny hoped) by the flippers and dorsal fin. He had been very careful to keep the straps clear of the single blowhole on the back of the head, through which the dolphin breathed when it surfaced, and which closed automatically when it dived.

Johnny attached the two nylon traces to the harness and gave them a good tug. Everything seemed to be staying in place, so he fastened the other ends to Mick's surf-board and climbed on top of it.

There was an ironic cheer from the crowd as Susie pulled him away from shore. She had needed no orders; with her usual grasp of the situation, she understood exactly what Johnny was trying to do.

He let her drag him out for a hundred yards, then pressed the LEFT button on the communicator. Susie responded at once; he tried RIGHT, and again she obeyed. The surf-board was already moving faster than he could have swum, yet the dolphin was barely exerting herself.

They were heading straight out to sea, when Johnny muttered, 'I'll show them!' and signalled FAST. The board gave a little jump and started to fly across the waves as Susie went into top gear. Johnny slid back a little, so that the board planed properly and did not nose down into the water. He felt very excited and proud of himself, and wondered how fast he was travelling. Flat out, Susie could do at least thirty miles an hour; even with the drag of the board and the restriction of the harness, she was probably touching fifteen or twenty. And that was quite a speed, when you were lying flat on the water with the spray blowing in your face.

There was a sudden 'snap', the board jerked wildly to one side, and Johnny flew to the other. When he came to the surface, spluttering, he found that nothing had broken; Susie had just popped out of her harness like a cork out of a bottle.

Well, one expected these little technical difficulties on the first trials. Though it was a long swim back to shore, where lots of people would be waiting to pull his leg, Johnny felt quite content. He had acquired a new mastery over the sea, that would allow him to roam the reef with far greater ease; and he had invented a new sport that would one day bring pleasure to thousands of men and dolphins alike.

Fifteen

Professor Kazan was delighted when he heard of Johnny's invention; it fell neatly into line with his own plans. Those plans were still rather vague, but they were beginning to take shape, and in another few weeks he would be able to go to his Advisory Committee with some ideas that would really make it sit up.

The Professor was not one of those scientists – like some pure mathematicians – who are unhappy if their work turns out to be of practical value. Though he would be quite content to study the dolphin language for the rest of his life, without attempting to use his knowledge, he knew that the time had come to apply it. The dolphins themselves had forced his hand.

He still had no idea what could, or even what *should*, be done about the killer whale problem. But he knew very well that if the dolphins expected to get much help from mankind, they would have to prove that they could do something in return.

As far back as the 1960s, Dr John Lilly, the first scientist to attempt communication with dolphins, had suggested ways in which they might co-operate with man. They could rescue survivors from shipwrecks – as they had demonstrated with Johnny – and they could help immeasurably in extending knowledge of the oceans. They must know of creatures never seen by man, and they might even settle the still-unsolved mystery of the Great Sea Serpent. If they would help fishermen on a large scale, as they had done occasionally on a small one, they might play an important role in feeding the Earth's six billion hungry mouths.

All these ideas were worth investigating, and Professor Kazan had some new ideas of his own. There was not a wreck in the world's oceans that dolphins could not locate and examine, down to their ultimate diving depth of at least a thousand feet. Even when a ship had been broken up centuries ago and covered with mud or coral, they could still spot it. They had a wonderfully developed sense of smell – or, rather, of taste – and could detect faint traces of metal, oil, or wood in the water. Dolphin trackers, sniffing like bloodhounds across the sea-bed, might revolutionize marine archaeology. Professor Kazan sometimes wondered, a little wistfully, if they could be trained to follow the scent of gold . . .

When he was ready to test some of his theories, the *Flying Fish* sailed north, carrying Einar, Peggy, Susie, and Sputnik in newly installed tanks. She also carried a good deal of special equipment; but she did not, to his bitter disappointment, carry Johnny. OSCAR had forbidden it.

'I'm sorry, Johnny,' said the Professor, glumly examining the typed card that the computer had flicked at him. 'You've A for Biology, A-minus for Chemistry, B-plus for Physics, and only B-minus for English, Mathematics and History. That really isn't good enough. How much time do you spend diving?'

'I didn't go out at all yesterday,' Johnny answered evasively.

'Since it never stopped raining, I'm not surprised. I'm thinking of the *average* day.'

'Oh, a couple of hours.'

'Morning *and* afternoon, I'm quite sure. Well, OSCAR has worked out a new schedule for you, concentrating on your bad subjects. I'm afraid you'll slip back even further if you come cruising with us. We'll be gone two weeks, and you can't afford to lose any more time.'

And that was that. It was no good arguing, even if he dared, for he knew that the Professor was right. In some ways, a coral island was the worst place in the world to study.

*

It was a long two weeks before the *Flying Fish* came back, after making several stops at the mainland. She had gone as far north as Cooktown, where the great Captain Cook had landed in 1770 to repair his damaged *Endeavour*.

From time to time, news of the expedition's progress came over the radio, but Johnny did not hear the full story until Mick reported to him on his return. The fact that Mick had gone on the voyage was a great help to Johnny's studies, for there was no one to lure him away from his tutors and teaching machines. He made remarkable progress in that two weeks, and the Professor was very pleased.

The first souvenir of the trip that Mick showed Johnny was a cloudy-white stone, slightly egg shaped and the size of a small pea.

99

'What is it?' asked Johnny, unimpressed.

'Don't you *know*?' said Mick. 'It's a pearl. And quite a good one.'

Johnny still didn't think much of it, but he had no desire to hurt Mick's feelings – or to show his ignorance.

'Where did you find it?' he asked.

'I didn't; Peggy got it, from eighty fathoms in the Marlin Deep. No diver's ever worked there – it's too dangerous, even with modern gear. But once after Uncle Henry had gone down in shallow water and showed them what silver-lip oysters were like, Peggy and Susie and Einar pulled up several hundred-weight. The Prof says it'll pay for this trip.'

'What – this pearl?'

'No, stupid – the shell. It's still the best stuff for buttons and knife handles, and the oyster farms can't supply enough of it. The Prof believes one could run a nice little pearl-shell industry with a few hundred trained dolphins.'

'Did you find any wrecks?'

'About twenty, though most of them were already marked on the Admiralty charts. But the big experiment was with the fishing trawlers out of Gladstone; we managed to drive two schools of tuna right into their nets.'

'I bet they were pleased.'

'Well, not as much as you might think. They wouldn't believe the dolphins did it – they claimed it was done by their own electric control fields and sound baits. We know better, and we'll prove it when we get some more dolphins trained. Then we'll be able to drive fish just where we like.'

Suddenly, Johnny remembered what Professor Kazan had said to him about dolphins, at their very first meeting. 'They have more freedom than we can ever know on land. They don't belong to anyone, and I hope they never will.'

Were they now about to lose that freedom, and would the

Professor himself, for all his good intentions, be the instrument of their loss?

Only the future could tell; but perhaps dolphins had never been as free as men had imagined. For Johnny could not forget the story of that killer whale, with twenty of the People of the Sea in its stomach.

One had to pay for liberty, as for everything else. Perhaps the dolphins would be willing to trade with mankind, exchanging some of their freedom for security. That was a choice that many nations had had to make, and the bargain had not always been a good one.

Professor Kazan, of course, had already thought of this, and much more. He was not worried, for he was still experimenting and collecting information. The decision had yet to be made; the treaty between man and dolphin, which he dimly envisaged, was still far in the future. It might not even be signed in his lifetime – if, indeed, one could expect dolphins to sign a treaty. But why not? Their mouths were wonderfully dextrous, as they had shown when collecting and transporting those hundreds of silver-lip pearl shells. Teaching dolphins to write, or at least to draw, was another of the Professor's long-term projects.

One which would take even longer – perhaps centuries – was the History of the Sea. Professor Kazan had always suspected – and now he was certain – that dolphins had marvellous memories. There had been a time, before the invention of writing, when men had carried their own past in their brains. Minstrels and bards memorized millions of words and passed them on from generation to generation. The songs they sang – the legends of gods and heroes and great battles before the beginning of history – were a mixture of fact and imagination. But the facts were there, if one could dig them out – as, in the nineteenth century, Schliemann dug Troy out of its three thousand years of rubble and proved that Homer had spoken the truth.

The dolphins also had their story-tellers, though the Professor had not yet contacted one. Einar had been able to repeat, in rough outline, some of their tales, which he had heard in his youth. Professor Kazan's translations had convinced him that these dolphin legends contained a wealth of information that could be found nowhere else. They went back earlier than any human myths or folk tales, for some of them contained clear references to the Ice Ages – and the last of those was seventeen thousand years ago.

And there was one tale so extraordinary that Professor Kazan had not trusted his own interpretation of the tape. He had given it to Dr Keith and asked him to make an independent analysis.

It had taken Keith, who was nothing like as good at translating Dolphin as was the Professor, nearly a month to make some sense of the story. Even then, he was so reluctant to give his version that Professor Kazan practically had to drag it out of him.

'It's a very old legend,' he began. 'Einar repeats that several times. And it seems to have made a great impression on the dolphins, for they emphasize that nothing like it ever happened before or afterward.

'As I understand it, there was a school of dolphins swimming at night off a large island, when it suddenly became like day and "the sun came down from the sky". I'm quite sure of *that* phrase. The "sun" landed in the water and went out; at least, it became dark again. But there was an enormous object floating on the sea – as long as 128 dolphins. Am I right so far?'

Professor Kazan nodded.

'I agree with everything except the number. I made it 256,

but that's not important. The thing was *big*, there's no doubt of that.'

Dolphins, the Professor had discovered, counted on a scale of two. This was just what one might expect, for they had only two 'fingers', or flippers, to count with. Their words for 1, 10, 100, 1,000, 10,000 corresponded to 1, 2, 4, 8, 16 in man's decimal notation. So to them, 128 and 256 were nice round numbers, signifying approximations, not exact measurements.

'The dolphins were frightened, and kept away from the thing,' continued Dr Keith. 'As it lay in the water, it made strange noises. Einar imitates some of them; to me they sound like electric motors or compressors at work.'

Professor Kazan nodded his agreement, but did not interrupt.

'Then there was a tremendous explosion, and the sea became boiling-hot. Everyone within 1,024, or even 2,048 lengths of the object was killed. It sank quickly, and there were more explosions as it went down.

'Even the dolphins who escaped without injury died soon afterwards, of an unknown disease. For years, everyone kept away from the area, but as nothing else happened, some inquisitive dolphins went back to investigate. They found a "place of many caves" resting on the sea bed, and hunted inside it for fish. And then these later visitors died of the same strange disease, so now no one goes near the spot. I think the main purpose of the story is to act as a warning.'

'A warning that's been repeated for thousands of years,' agreed the Professor. 'And a warning against *what*?'

Dr Keith stirred uneasily in his chair. 'I don't see any way out,' he said. 'If that legend is based on fact – and it's hard to see how the dolphins could have invented it – a spaceship landed somewhere a few thousand years ago. Then its nuclear engines blew up, poisoning the sea with radioactivity. It's a fantastic theory, but I can't think of a better explanation.'

'Why is it fantastic?' asked Professor Kazan. 'We're certain now that there is plenty of intelligent life in the universe, so we'd expect other races to build spaceships. In fact, it's been difficult to explain why they *haven't* come to Earth before now.

'Some scientists consider that we probably did have visitors in the past, but they came so many thousands of years ago that there's no evidence for it. Well, now we may have some evidence.'

'What are you going to do about it?'

'There's nothing we can do at the moment. I've questioned Einar, and he hasn't any idea where all this happened. We must get hold of one of those dolphin minstrels and record the complete saga. Let's hope that it gives more details. Once we know the approximate area, we should be able to pinpoint the wreck with Geiger counters – even after ten thousand years. There's only one thing I'm afraid of.'

'What's that?'

'The killer whales may have swallowed the information first. And then we'll never know the truth.'

Sixteen

No visitor to the island had ever been welcomed with such mixed feelings. Everyone not out at sea was gathered around the pool when the big cargo-copter came flying in from the

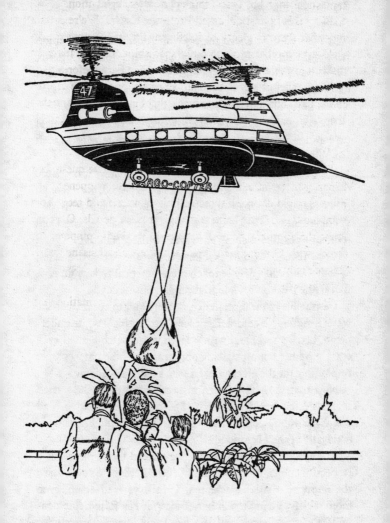

South, all the way from the Tasmanian Whale Research Station.

It hovered high above the pool, the downblast of its rotors tearing the surface of the water into fantastic, shifting patterns. Then the hatches in its belly opened, and a large sling slowly descended. When it hit the pool, there was a sudden eruption, a great flurry of spray and foam – and the sling was empty.

But the pool was not. Cruising around it on a swift voyage of exploration was the largest and fiercest creature ever to visit Dolphin Island.

Yet at his first sight of the killer whale, Johnny was a little disappointed. It was smaller than he had expected, even though it was far bigger than any dolphin. He mentioned his disappointment to Mick, when the cargo-copter had departed and it became possible to speak once again without shouting.

'It's a female,' said Mick. 'They're half the size of the males. Which means that they're much more practical to keep in captivity. She'll eat only a hundredweight of fish a day.'

Despite his natural prejudice, Johnny had to admit that she was a handsome creature. Her piebald colouring – white underneath, black above, and with a large white patch behind each eye – gave her a most striking appearance. These patches were responsible for the nickname she soon acquired – Snowy.

Now that she had finished inspecting the pool, she started to survey the world around it. She reared her massive head out of the water, looked at the crowd with keen, intelligent eyes, and lazily opened her mouth.

At the sight of those terrible, peg-shaped teeth, there was a respectful murmur from the audience. Perhaps Snowy knew the impression she had created, for she yawned again, even more widely, giving a still better view of her formidable dentures. Dolphins have small, pin-like teeth, intended merely for grasping fish before they are swallowed whole, but *these* teeth were designed to do the same job as a shark's. They could bite clean through a seal or a dolphin – or a man.

Now that the island had acquired a killer whale, everyone wanted to see what the Professor would do with her. For the first three days, he left her alone, until she had become used to her new surroundings and had recovered from the excitement of the trip. Since she had already been in captivity for several months, and was quite used to human beings, she quickly settled down and accepted both live and dead fish when they were given to her.

The task of feeding the whale was undertaken by Mick's family, usually by his father Jo Nauru or his uncle Stephen, skipper of the *Flying Fish*. Though they took on the job merely to earn some extra money, they soon became quite fond of their charge. She was intelligent, which everyone had expected, but she was also good-natured – which hardly seemed right for a killer whale. Mick grew particularly attached to her, and she showed obvious pleasure when he came near the pool – and disappointment if he left without giving her anything.

When he was quite sure that Snowy had settled down and was taking a healthy interest in life, the Professor began his first tests. He played some simple phrases of Dolphin to her through the underwater hydrophones, and studied her reactions.

At first, they were quite violent. She charged around the pool in all directions, looking for the source of the noise. There was no doubt that she associated dolphin voices with food, and thought that dinner had been served.

It took her only a few minutes to realize that she had been fooled and that there weren't any dolphins in the pool. After that, she listened attentively to the sounds that were played to her, but refused to go chasing after them. Professor Kazan's hope that she would reply to some of the Dolphin talk in her own language was not fulfilled; she remained stubbornly dumb.

Nevertheless, he was making a little progress in 'Orcan', using tape recordings of killer-whale sounds. He used OSCAR's infallible computer memory to hunt through the mass of material for Dolphin words. He found many. The names of several fish, for example, were almost the same in Orcan as in Dolphin. Probably both languages – like English and German, or French and Italian – sprang from some common ancient origin. Professor Kazan hoped so, for it would greatly simplify his work.

He was not too disappointed by Snowy's lack of co-operation, for he had other plans for her, which could be carried out whether she co-operated or not. After she had been on the island for two weeks, a team of medical technicians arrived from India and began to install electronic equipment at the edge of the pool. When they were ready, the water was drained off, and the indignant whale was stranded helplessly in the shallows.

The next step involved ten men, some strong ropes, and a massive wooden framework that had been designed to hold the whale's head clamped in a fixed position. She was not at all pleased with this, nor was Mick, who had to assist with the project by playing a hose pipe over Snowy to prevent her skin from drying in the sun.

'No one's going to hurt you, old girl,' he said reassuringly. 'It'll all be over in a minute, and you can start swimming round again.'

Then, to Mick's alarm, one of the technicians approached Snowy with an object that looked like a cross between a hypodermic needle and an electric drill. With great care, he selected a spot on the back of the whale's head, placed the device against it, and pressed a button. There was a faint, high-pitched whine, and the needle sank deep into Snowy's brain, going through the thick bone of the skull as effortlessly as a hot knife through butter.

The operation upset Mick much more than it did Snowy, who seemed scarcely aware of the pinprick. This would not have surprised anyone with a knowledge of physiology, but Mick, like most people, did not know the curious fact that the brain has no sense of feeling. It can be cut or pierced without any discomfort to its owner.

Altogether, ten probes were sunk into Snowy's brain. Wires were connected to them and taken to a flat, streamlined box that was clamped to the top of the whale's head. The whole operation took less than an hour. When it was over, the pool was flooded again and Snowy, puffing and blowing, started to swim lazily back and forth. She was obviously none the worse for her experience, though it seemed to Mick that she looked at him with the hurt expression of a person who had been let down by a trusted friend.

The next day, Dr Saha arrived from New Delhi. As a member of the Institute's Advisory Committee, he was an old friend of Professor Kazan's. He was also a world authority on that most complex of all organs, the human brain.

'The last time I used this equipment,' said the physiologist, as he watched Snowy swimming back and forth in the pool, 'it was on an elephant. Before I'd finished, I could control his trunk accurately enough to type with it.'

'We don't need that sort of virtuosity here,' Professor Kazan answered. 'All I want to do is to control Snowy's movements and to teach her not to eat dolphins.'

'If my men have put the electrodes in the right area, I think I can promise that. But not immediately; I'll have to do some brain-mapping first.'

This 'brain-mapping' was slow, delicate work, requiring great patience and skill, and Saha sat for hours at his instrument panel, observing Snowy's behaviour as she dived, basked in the sun, swam lazily around the pool, or took the fish that Mick offered her. All the time her brain was broadcasting like a satellite in orbit, through the radio transmitter attached to it. The impulses picked up by the probes were recorded on tape, so that Dr Saha could see the pattern of electrical activity corresponding to any particular action.

At last he was ready for the first step. Instead of receiving impulses from Snowy's brain, he began to feed electric currents *into* it.

The result was both fascinating and uncanny – more like magic than science. By turning a knob or closing a switch, Dr Saha could make the great animal swim to right or left, describe circles or figure eights, float motionless in the centre of the pool, or carry out any other movement he wished. Johnny's efforts to control Sputnik and Susie with the communicator, which had once seemed so impressive, now appeared almost childish.

But Johnny did not mind, Susie and Sputnik were his friends, and he preferred to leave them freedom of choice. If they did not wish to obey him – as was often the case – that was their privilege. Snowy had no alternative; the electric currents fed into her brain had turned her into a living robot, with no will of her own, compelled to carry out the orders Dr Saha gave her.

The more that Johnny thought about this, the more uncomfortable he became. Could the same control be applied to me? When he made inquiries, he found that this had indeed been done, many times, in laboratory experiments. Here was a scientific tool that might be as dangerous as atomic energy if used for evil instead of good.

There was no doubt that Professor Kazan intended to use it for good – at least, for the good of dolphins – but *how* he intended to use it still puzzled Johnny. He was not very much wiser even when the experiment moved into its next stage, with the arrival on the island of a most peculiar object – a life-size mechanical dolphin, driven by electric motors.

It had been built twenty years ago by a scientist at the Naval Research Laboratories, who couldn't understand how dolphins managed to swim as fast as they did. According to his calculations, their muscles should not be able to drive them at much more than ten miles an hour – yet they could cruise comfortably at twice that speed.

So the scientist had built a model dolphin and studied its behaviour as it swam up and down, loaded with instruments. The project had been a failure, but the model was so beautifully made and performed so well that no one had had the heart to destroy it, even when its designer had given up in disgust. From time to time the Lab technicians dusted it off for public demonstrations, and thus the Professor had come to hear of it. In its small way, it was quite famous.

It would have fooled any human observer, but when it was lowered into Snowy's tank, before scores of fascinated spectators, the result was an utter anticlimax. The whale took one contemptuous glance at the mechanical toy and then ignored it completely.

'Just what I was afraid of,' said the Professor, without too much disappointment. Like all scientists, he had long ago learned that most experiments are failures, and he was not ashamed to make a fool of himself, even in public. (After all, the great Darwin once spent hours playing the trumpet in a vegetable garden, to see if sound affected plant growth.) 'She probably heard the electric motor and knew the thing was a fake. Well, there's no alternative. We'll have to use real dolphins as bait.'

'Are you going to call for volunteers?' asked Dr Saha, jokingly.

The joke, however, back-fired on him. Professor Kazan considered the suggestion carefully, then nodded his head in agreement.

'I'll do exactly that,' he said.

Seventeen

'There's a general feeling around the island,' said Mick, 'that the Prof has gone stark, staring mad.'

'You know that's nonsense,' retorted Johnny, springing to the defence of his hero. 'What's he done now?'

'He's been using that brain-wave gadget to control Snowy's feeding. He tells me to offer her one kind of fish, and then Dr Saha stops her from eating it; after he's given her several jabs, she doesn't even try any more. He calls it "conditioning". Now there are four or five big jacks swimming round in the pool, but she won't look at them. She'll eat any other fish, though.'

'Why does that make the Prof crazy?'

'Well, it's obvious what he's up to. If he can keep Snowy from eating jacks, he can keep her from eating dolphins. But what good will *that* be? There are millions of killer whales — he can't condition them all!'

'Whatever the Prof's doing,' said Johnny stubbornly, 'there's a good reason for it. Wait and see.'

'All the same, I wish they'd stop bothering Snowy. I'm afraid it'll make her bad-tempered.'

That was an odd thing to say about a killer whale, thought Johnny.

'I don't see that *that* matters very much,' he said.

Mick grinned rather shamefacedly and scuffed the ground with his feet.

'You promise you won't tell anyone?' he asked.

'Of course.'

'Well, I've been swimming with her a good deal. She's more fun than your little tadpoles.'

Johnny stared at him in utter amazement, quite ignoring the insult to Susie and Sputnik.

'And you said the Professor was mad!' he exclaimed, when he had got his breath back. 'You aren't pulling my leg again, are you?' he added suspiciously. By now he could usually spot one of Mick's jokes, but this time he seemed to be serious.

Mick shook his head.

'If you don't believe me, come down to the pool. Oh, I know it sounds crazy, but it's really quite safe. The whole thing started by accident: I got careless one day when I was feeding Snowy, slipped on the edge of the pool, and fell in.'

'Phew!' whistled Johnny. 'Bet you thought your last moment had come!'

'I sure did. When I came up, I was looking straight into Snowy's mouth.' He paused. 'You know, it isn't true about recalling your past life at moments like this. All I thought about was those teeth. I wondered if I'd go down in one piece, or whether she'd bite me in two.'

'And what happened?' asked Johnny breathlessly.

'Well, she *didn't* bite me in two. She just gave me a gentle nudge with her nose, as if to say, "Let's be friends". And that's what we've been ever since. If I don't go swimming with her every day, she gets very upset. Sometimes it's not easy to manage, because if anyone sees me, they'll tell the Prof, and that'll be the end of it.'

He laughed at Johnny's expression, which was a mixture of alarm and disapproval.

'It's a lot safer than lion-taming, and men have been doing that for years. I get quite a kick out of it, too. Maybe someday I'll work up to the big whales, like a hundred-and-fifty-ton Blue.'

'Well, at least one of those couldn't swallow you,' said Johnny, who had learned a good deal about whales since coming to the island. 'Their throats are too small – they can eat only shrimps and little things like that.'

'All right then – what about a sperm whale – Moby Dick himself? *He* can swallow a thirty-foot squid in one gulp.'

As Mick warmed to his theme, Johnny slowly realized that he was motivated by straightforward envy. Even now, the dolphins merely tolerated him and never showed any of the affectionate delight they showered upon Johnny. He felt glad that Mick had at last found a cetacean friend, but wished it had been a more sensible one.

As it happened, he never had a chance to see Mick and Snowy swimming together, for Professor Kazan was now ready for his next experiment. He had been working for days, splicing tapes and composing long sentences in Dolphin; even now he was not certain whether he could convey the exact meaning he wanted to. He hoped that in the parts where his translation fell down, the intelligence of the dolphins would bridge the gap.

He often wondered what they thought of his conversation, built up of words from many different sources. Each sentence he broadcast into the water must sound as if there were a dozen or more dolphins, each taking his turn to speak a few words in a different accent. It must be very puzzling to his listeners, since they could hardly imagine such things as tape recording and sound-editing. The fact that they made any sense at all out of his noises was a tribute both to their intelligence and their patience.

As the *Flying Fish* pulled away from her moorings, Professor Kazan was unusually nervous.

'Do you know what I feel like?' he said to Dr Keith as they stood on the foredeck together. 'It's as if I'd invited my friends to a party, just to let loose a man-eating tiger among them.'

'It's not as bad as that,' laughed Keith. 'You've given them fair warning, and you do have the tiger under control.'

'I *hope*,' said the Professor.

Somewhere on board, a loud-speaker announced: 'They're opening the pool gate now. She doesn't seem in a hurry to leave.'

Professor Kazan raised a pair of binoculars and stared back at the island.

'I don't want Saha to control her until we have to,' he said. 'Ah, here she comes.'

Snowy was moving down the channel from the pool, swimming very slowly. When the channel came to an end and she found herself in open water, she seemed quite bewildered and turned around several times as if finding her bearings. It was a typical reaction of an animal – or a man – that had spent a long time in captivity and had now been turned loose into the great outside world.

'Give her a call,' said the Professor. The Dolphin 'COME HERE!' signal went out through the water; even if the phrase was not the same in Snowy's own language, it was one of those that she understood. She began to swim towards the *Flying Fish* and kept up with the boat as it drew away from the island, heading out for the deeper water beyond the reef.

'I want plenty of room to manoeuvre,' said Professor Kazan.

'And I'm sure Einar, Peggy and Co., would prefer it that way – just in case they have to run.'

'*If* they come. Perhaps they'll have more sense,' Dr Keith answered doubtfully.

'Well, we'll know in a few minutes. The broadcast has been going out all morning, so every dolphin for miles around must have heard it.'

'Look!' said Keith suddenly, pointing to the west. Half a mile away, a small school of dolphins was swimming parallel to the ship's course. 'There are your volunteers, and it doesn't look as if they're in a hurry to come closer.'

'This is where the fun begins,' muttered the Professor. 'Let's join Saha up on the bridge.'

The radio equipment that sent out the signals to the box on Snowy's head, and received her brain impulses in return, had been set up near the wheel. This made the *Flying Fish*'s little bridge very crowded, but direct contact between skipper Stephen Nauru and Dr Saha was essential. Both men knew exactly what to do, and Professor Kazan had no intention of interfering, except in case of emergency.

'Snowy's spotted them,' whispered Keith.

There was no doubt of that. Gone now was the uncertainty she had shown when first released; she began to move like a speed-boat, leaving a foaming wake behind her as she headed straight for the dolphins.

Understandably, they scattered. With a guilty twinge, the Professor wondered just what they were thinking about him at this moment, that is, if they were thinking of anything except Snowy.

She was only thirty feet from one sleek, plump dolphin when she shot into the air, landed with a crash in the water, and lay there motionless, shaking her head in an almost human manner.

'Two volts, central punishment area,' said Dr Saha, taking his finger off the button. 'Wonder if she'll try it again?'

The dolphins, doubtless surprised and impressed by the demonstration, had re-formed a few hundred yards away. They, too, were motionless in the water, with their heads all turned watchfully towards their ancient enemy.

Snowy was getting over her shock and beginning to move once more. This time she swam quite slowly and did not head towards the dolphins at all. It was some time before the watchers understood her tactics.

She was swimming in a wide circle, with the still motionless dolphins at its centre. One had to look closely to see that the circle was slowly contracting.

'Thinks she can fool us, does she?' said Professor Kazan admiringly. 'I expect she'll get as close as she dares, pretending she's not interested, and then make a dash for it.'

This was exactly what she did do. The fact that the dolphins stood their ground for so long was an impressive proof of their confidence in their human friends, and yet another demonstration of the amazing speed at which they learned. It was seldom necessary to tell a dolphin anything twice.

The tension grew as Snowy spiralled inwards, like an old-time gramophone pick-up tracking in towards the spindle. She was only forty feet from the nearest, and bravest, dolphin when she made her bid.

A killer whale can accelerate at an unbelievable speed. But Dr Saha was ready, his finger only a fraction of an inch from the button. Snowy didn't have a chance.

She was an intelligent animal – not quite as intelligent as her would-be victims, but almost in the same class. She knew that she was beaten. When she recovered from the second shock, she turned her back on the dolphins and started to swim directly away from them. As she did so, Dr Saha's finger darted towards his panel once more.

'Hey, what are you up to?' asked the *Flying Fish*'s skipper, who had been watching all this with disapproval. Like his nephew Mick, he did not care to see Snowy pushed around. 'Isn't she doing what you want?'

'I'm not punishing her – I'm rewarding her,' explained Dr Saha. 'As long as I keep this button down, she's having a perfectly wonderful time, because I'm putting a few volts into the pleasure-centres of her brain.'

'I think that's enough for one day,' Professor Kazan said. 'Send her back to the pool – she's earned her lunch.'

'The same thing tomorrow, Professor?' asked the skipper as *Flying Fish* headed for home.

'Yes, Steve – the same every day. But I'll be surprised if we have to keep it up for more than a week.'

In fact, after only three days it was obvious that Snowy had learned her lesson. It was no longer necessary to punish her, only to reward her with short spells of electrical ecstasy. The dolphins lost their fears equally fast, and at the end of a week, they and Snowy were completely at ease with each other. They would hunt around the reef together, sometimes co-operating to trap a school of fish, sometimes foraging independently. A few of the younger dolphins even started their usual horseplay around Snowy, who showed neither annoyance nor uncontrollable hunger when they bumped against her.

On the seventh day, Snowy was not steered back to her pool after her morning romp with the dolphins.

'We've done all we can,' said the Professor. 'I'm going to turn her loose.'

'Isn't that taking a risk?' objected Dr Keith.

'Of course it is, but we've got to take it sooner or later. Unless we let her run wild again we'll never know how well her conditioning will last.'

'And if she does make a snack of a few dolphins – what then?'

'The rest of them will tell us, soon enough. Then we'll go

out and round her up again. She'll be easy to locate with that radio pack she's carrying.'

Stephen Nauru, who had been listening to the conversation as he stood at *Flying Fish*'s wheel, looked back over his shoulder and asked the question that was worrying everybody.

'Even if you turned Snowy into a vegetarian, what about the other millions of the beasts?'

'We mustn't be impatient, Steve,' answered the Professor. 'I'm still only collecting information, and none of this may ever be the slightest use to man or dolphin. But I'm certain of one thing – the whole talkative dolphin world must know of this experiment by now, and they'll realize that we're doing our best for them. A good bargaining point for your fishermen.'

'Hmm – I hadn't thought of that one.'

'Anyway, if this works with Snowy, I've a theory that we need condition only a few killers in any one area. And only females – they'll teach their mates and their offspring that if you eat a dolphin, you'll get the most horrible headache.'

Steve was not convinced. Had he realized the tremendous, irresistible power of electric brain-stimulation, he might have been more impressed.

'I still don't think one vegetarian could make a tribe of cannibals mend their ways,' he said.

'You may be quite right,' answered the Professor. 'That's what I want to find out. Even if the job's possible at all, it may not be worth doing. And even if it's worth doing, it may take several lifetimes. But one has to be an optimist; don't you remember the history of the twentieth century?'

'Which bit of it?' asked Steve. 'There was rather a lot.'

'The only bit that really matters. Fifty years ago, a great many people refused to believe that all the *human* nations could live in peace. Well, you know that they were wrong; if they'd been right, you and I wouldn't be here. So don't be too pessimistic about this project.'

Suddenly, Steve burst into laughter.

'Now what's so funny?' asked the Professor.

'I was just thinking,' said Steve, 'that it's been thirty years since they had an excuse for awarding the Nobel Peace Prize. If this plan of yours comes off, you'll be in the running.'

Eighteen

While Professor Kazan experimented and dreamed, forces were gathering in the Pacific that cared nothing for the hopes and fears either of men or of dolphins. Mick and Johnny were among the first to glimpse their power, one moonless night out on the reef.

As usual, they were hunting for crayfish and rare shells, and this time Mick had acquired a new tool to help him. It was a watertight flashlight, somewhat larger than normal, and when Mick switched it on, it produced a very faint blue glow.

But it also produced a powerful beam of ultra-violet light, invisible to the human eye. When this fell upon many varieties of corals and shells, they seemed to burst into fire, blazing with fluorescent blues and golds and greens in the darkness. The invisible beam was a magic wand, revealing objects that were otherwise hidden and that could not be seen even by ordinary light. Where the sand had been disturbed by a burrowing mollusc, for example, the ultra-violet beam betrayed the tiny furrow – and Mick had another victim.

Underwater, the effect was astonishing. When the boys dived in the coral pools near the edge of the reef, the dim blue light sliced ahead for fantastic distances. They could see corals fluorescing a dozen yards away, like stars or nebulae in the deeps of space. The natural luminosity of the sea, beautiful and striking though it was, could not compare with this.

Fascinated by their wonderful new toy, Mick and Johnny dived longer than they had intended. When they prepared to go home, they found that the weather had changed.

Until now, the night had been calm and still, the only sound the murmur of the waves, lazily rolling against the reef. But in the last hour a wind had come up, blowing in fitful gusts, and the voice of the sea had acquired an angrier, more determined note.

Johnny saw the thing first, as he was climbing out of the pool. Beyond the reef, at a distance that was quite impossible to judge, a faint light was moving slowly across the waters. For a moment he wondered if it could be a ship; then he realized that it was too blurred and formless, like a luminous fog.

'Mick,' he whispered urgently, 'what's *that*, out there at sea?'

Mick's answer was not reassuring. He gave a low whistle of astonishment and moved closer to Johnny, as if for protection.

Almost unable to believe their eyes, they watched as the mist gathered itself together, became brighter and more sharp-edged, and climbed higher and higher in the sky. Within a few minutes, it was no longer a faint glow in the darkness: it was a pillar of fire walking upon the face of the sea.

It filled them both with superstitious awe – with the fear of the unknown, which men will never lose, because the wonders of the universe are without end. Their minds were full of wild explanations, fantastic theories – and then Mick gave a relieved, though rather shaken, laugh.

'I know what that is,' he said. 'It's only a water-spout. I've seen them before, but never at night.'

Like many mysteries, the explanation was simple – once you knew it. But the wonder remained, and the boys stared in fascination at the spinning column of water as it sucked up billions of the sea's luminous creatures and scattered them into the sky. It must have been many miles away, for Johnny could not hear the roar of its passage over the waves; and presently it vanished in the direction of the mainland.

When the boys had recovered from their astonishment, the incoming tide had risen to their knees.

'If we don't get a move on, we'll have to swim for it,' said Mick. Then he added thoughtfully, as he splashed off towards the island, 'I don't like the look of that thing. It's a sign of bad weather – bet you ten to one we're in for a big blow.'

How true that was they began to realize by next morning. Even if one knew nothing about meteorology, the picture on the television screen was terrifying. A great whirlpool of cloud, a thousand miles across, covered all the western Pacific. As seen from the weather satellite's cameras, looking down upon it from far out in space, it appeared to be quite motionless. But that was only because of its size. If one watched carefully, one could see after a few minutes that the spiral bands of cloud were sweeping swiftly across the face of the globe. The winds that drove them were moving at speeds up to a hundred and fifty miles an hour, for this was the greatest hurricane to strike the Queensland coast in a generation.

On Dolphin Island, no one wandered very far from a television screen. Every hour, revised forecasts came through from the computers that were predicting the progress of the storm, but there was little change during the day. Meteorology was now an exact science; the weathermen could state with confidence what was going to happen – though they could not, as yet, do much about it.

The island had known many other storms, and the prevailing mood was excitement and alertness, rather than alarm. Luckily, the tide would be out when the hurricane reached its peak, so there was no danger of waves sweeping over the island – as had happened elsewhere in the Pacific.

All through the day, Johnny was helping with the safety precautions. Nothing movable could be left in the open; windows had to be boarded over and boats drawn up as far as possible on the beach. The *Flying Fish* was secured to four heavy anchors, and to make doubly certain that she did not move, ropes were taken from her and secured to a group of pandanus trees on the island. Most of the fishermen, however, were not much worried about their boats, for the harbour was on the sheltered side of the island. The forest would break the full force of the gale.

The day was hot and oppressive, without a breath of wind. It scarcely needed the picture on the television screen and the steady flow of weather reports from the east, to know that Nature was planning one of her big productions. Moreover, though the sky was clear and cloudless, the storm had sent its messages ahead of it. All day long, tremendous waves had been battering against the outer reef, until the whole island shook beneath their impact.

When darkness fell, the sky was still clear and the stars seemed abnormally brilliant. Johnny was standing outside the Naurus' concrete-and-aluminium bungalow, taking a last look at the sky before turning in, when he became aware of a new sound above the thunder of the waves. It was a sound such as he had never heard before, as of a monstrous animal moaning in pain, and even on that hot, sultry evening, it seemed to chill his blood.

123

And then he saw something to the east that broke his nerve completely. An unbroken wall of utter blackness was riding up the sky, climbing visibly even as he watched. He had heard and seen the onset of the hurricane, and he did not wait for more.

'I was just coming to get you,' said Mick, when Johnny closed the door thankfully behind him. Those were the last words that he heard for many hours.

Seconds later, the whole house gave a shudder. Then came a noise which, despite its incredible violence, was startlingly familiar. For a moment it took Johnny back to the very beginning of his adventures; he remembered the thunder of the *Santa Anna* jets, only a few feet beneath him, as he climbed aboard the hovership, half a world away and a seeming lifetime ago.

The roar of the hurricane had already made speech impossible. Yet now, unbelievably, the sound level became even higher, for such a deluge as Johnny had never imagined was descending upon the house. The feeble word 'rain' could not begin to describe it. Judging by the sound that was coming through roof and walls, a man in the open would be drowned by the sheer mass of descending water – if he was not crushed first.

Yet Mick's family was taking all this quite calmly. The younger children were even gathered around the television set, watching the pictures, though they could not hear a word of the sound. Mrs Nauru was placidly knitting – a rare accomplishment which she had learned in her youth and which normally fascinated Johnny because he had never seen anyone doing it before. But now he was too disturbed to watch the intricate movement of the needles and the magical transformation of wool into sock or sweater.

He tried to guess, from the uproar around him, what was happening outside. Surely, trees were being torn up by their roots; boats and even houses scattered by the gale! But the howl of the wind and the deafening, unending crash of water masked all other sounds. Guns might be booming outside the door, and no one would ever hear them.

Johnny looked at Mick for reassurance; he wanted some sign that everything was all right, that it would soon be over and everything would be normal. But Mick shrugged his shoulders, then made a pantomime of putting on a face-mask and breathing from an Aqualung mouthpiece, which Johnny did not think at all funny in the circumstances.

He wondered what was happening to the rest of the island, but somehow nothing seemed real except this one room and the people in it. It was as if they alone existed now, and the hurricane was launching its attack upon them personally. So might Noah and his family have waited for the flood to rise around them, the sole survivors of their world.

Johnny had never thought that a storm on land could frighten him; after all, it was 'only' wind and rain. But the demonic fury raving around the frail fortress in which he was sheltering was something beyond all his experience and imagination. If he had been told that the whole island was about to be blown into the sea, he would have believed it.

Suddenly, even above the roar of the storm, there came the sound of a mighty crash – though whether it was close at hand or far away it was impossible to tell. At the same instant, the lights went out.

That moment of utter darkness, at the height of the storm, was one of the most terrifying that Johnny had ever experienced. As long as he had been able to see his friends, even if he could not talk with them, he had felt reasonably safe. Now he was alone in the screaming night, helpless before natural forces that he had never known existed.

Luckily, the darkness lasted for only a few seconds. Mr Nauru had been expecting the worst; he had an electric lantern ready, and when its light came on, showing everything quite unchanged, Johnny felt ashamed of his fright.

Even in a hurricane, life continues. Now that they had lost the television, the younger children started to play with their toys or read picture books. Mrs Nauru continued placidly knitting, while her husband began to plough through a thick World Food Organization report on Australian fisheries, full of charts, statistics, and maps. When Mick set up a game of draughts, Johnny did not feel much like challenging him, but he realized that it was the sensible thing to do.

So the night dragged on. Sometimes the hurricane slackened for a moment, and the roar of the wind dropped to a level at which one could make oneself heard by shouting. But nobody made the effort, for there was nothing to say, and very quickly the noise returned to its former volume.

Around midnight, Mrs Nauru got up, disappeared into the kitchen, and came back a few minutes later with a jug of hot coffee, half a dozen tin mugs, and an assorted collection of cakes. Johnny wondered if this was the last snack he would ever eat; nevertheless, he enjoyed it, and then went on losing games to Mick.

Not until four in the morning, a bare two hours before dawn, did the fury of the storm begin to abate. Slowly its strength ebbed, until presently it was no more than an ordinary howling gale. At the same time the rain slackened, so that they no longer seemed to be living beneath a waterfall. Around five, there were a few isolated gusts, as violent as anything that had gone before, but they were the hurricane's dying spasms. By the time the sun rose over the battered island, it was possible to venture out of doors.

Johnny had expected disaster, and he was not disappointed. As he and Mick scrambled over the dozens of fallen trees that were blocking once familiar paths, they met the other islanders wandering around, like the dazed inhabitants of a bombed city. Many of them were injured, with heads bandaged or arms in slings, but by good planning and good luck, there had been no serious casualties.

The real damage was to property. All the power lines were down, but they could be quickly replaced. Much more serious was the fact that the electric generating plant was ruined. It had been wrecked by a tree that had not merely fallen, but had walked end-over-end for a hundred yards and then smashed into the power building like a giant club. Even the stand-by Diesel plant had been involved in the catastrophe.

There was worse to come. Some time during the night, defying all predictions, the wind had shifted around to the west and attacked the island from its normally sheltered side. Of the fishing fleet, half had been sunk, while the other half

had been hurled up on the beach and smashed into firewood. The *Flying Fish* lay on her side, partly submerged. She could be salvaged, but it would be weeks before she would sail again.

Yet despite all the ruin and havoc, no one seemed too depressed. At first Johnny was astonished by this; then he slowly came to understand the reason. Hurricanes were one of the basic, unavoidable facts of life on the Great Barrier Reef. Anyone who chose to make his home here must be prepared to pay the price. If he couldn't take it, he had a simple remedy; he could always move somewhere else.

Professor Kazan put it in a different way, when Johnny and Mick found him examining the blown-down fence around the dolphin pool.

'Perhaps this has put us back six months,' he said. 'But we'll get over it. Equipment can always be replaced – men and knowledge can't. And we've lost neither of those.'

'What about OSCAR?' Mick asked.

'Dead – until we get power again, but all his memory circuits are intact.'

That means no lessons for a while, thought Johnny. The ill wind had blown some good, after all.

But it had also blown more harm than anyone yet appreciated – anyone except Nurse Tessie. That large and efficient woman was now looking, with utter dismay, at the soaking wreckage of her medical stores.

Cuts, bruises, even broken limbs she could deal with, as she had been doing ever since dawn. But anything more serious was now beyond her control; she did not have even an ampoule of penicillin that she could trust.

In the cold and miserable aftermath of the storm, she could count on several chills and fevers and perhaps more serious complaints. Well, she had better waste no time radioing for fresh supplies.

Quickly, she made a list of the drugs which, she knew from earlier experience, she would be needing in the next few days. Then she hurried to the Message Centre, and received a second shock.

Two disheartened electronics technicians were toasting their soldering irons on a Primus stove. Around them was a shambles of wires and broken instrument racks, impaled by the branch of a pandanus tree that had come straight through the roof.

'Sorry, Tess,' they said. 'If we can contact the mainland by the end of the week, it'll be a miracle. We're back to smoke signals, from now.'

Tessie thought that over.

'I can't take any chances,' she said. 'We'll have to send a boat across.'

Both technicians laughed bitterly.

'Hadn't you *heard*?' said one. '*Flying Fish* is upside down, and all the other boats are in the middle of the island, parked in the trees.'

As Tessie absorbed this report – slightly, but only slightly, exaggerated – she felt more helpless than she had ever been since that time Matron had ticked her off as a raw probationer. She could only hope that everyone would keep healthy until communications were restored.

But by evening she had attended to one injured foot that looked gangrenous; and then the Professor, pale and shaky, came to see her.

'Tessie,' he said, 'you'd better take my temperature. I think I've got a fever.'

Before midnight, she was sure that it was pneumonia.

Nineteen

The news that Professor Kazan was seriously ill, and that there was no way of treating him adequately, caused more dismay than all the damage wrought by the hurricane. And it hit no one harder than Johnny.

Though he had never stopped to think about it, the island had become the home he had never known, and the Professor a replacement for the father he could scarcely remember. Here he had felt the security which he had longed for and unconsciously striven to find. Now that security was threatened because no one could get a message across a hundred miles of sea – in this age when moons and planets talked to one another.

Only a hundred miles! Why, he himself had travelled a greater distance, when he first came to the island . . .

And with that memory, he suddenly knew, beyond all doubt or argument, exactly what he had to do. Dolphins had brought him as far as Dolphin Island; now they could carry him the rest of the way to the mainland.

He was sure that Susie and Sputnik, taking turns in pulling the surfboard, could get him across that hundred miles of water in less than twelve hours. This would be the pay-off for all the days they had spent together, hunting and exploring along the edge of the reef. With the two dolphins beside him, he felt absolutely safe in the sea; they knew all his wishes, even without the use of the communicator.

Johnny looked back at some of the trips they had made together. With Susie towing Mick's large board, and Sputnik towing Johnny on a smaller one, they had once crossed to the adjacent reef on Wreck Island, which was about ten miles away. The journey had taken just over an hour – and the dolphins had not been hurrying.

But how could he convince anyone that this was not a crazy, suicidal stunt? Only Mick would understand. The other islanders would certainly stop him if they had any idea what he was planning. Well, he would have to get away before they knew.

Mick's reaction was just what he had expected. He took the plan perfectly seriously, but was not at all happy about it.

'I'm sure it can be done,' he said. 'But you can't go by yourself.'

Johnny shook his head.

'I've thought of that,' he answered. For the first time in his life, he felt glad that he was small. 'Remember those races we've had? How many have *you* won? You're too big – you'd only slow us down.'

That was perfectly true, and Mick could not deny it. Even the more powerful Susie could not tow him as fast as Sputnik could tow Johnny.

Defeated on this point, Mick tried a new argument.

'It's over twenty-four hours since we've been cut off from the mainland. Before long, someone's bound to fly over to see what's happened, since they've had no word from us. You may risk your neck for nothing.'

'That's true,' admitted Johnny. 'But whose neck is more important – mine or Professor Kazan's? If we keep on waiting, it may be too late. Besides, they'll be pretty busy on the mainland after that storm. It may be a week before they work around to us.'

'Tell you what,' said Mick. 'We'll get organized, and if there's no sign of help and the Professor's still bad by the time you're ready to go, then we'll talk it over again.'

'You won't speak to anyone?' said Johnny anxiously.

'Of course not. By the way, where *are* Susie and Sputnik? Are you sure you can find them?'

'Yes – they were around the jetty earlier this morning, looking for us. They'll come quickly enough when I push the HELP! button.'

Mick began to count items off on his fingers.

'You'll want a flask of water – one of those flat plastic ones – some concentrated food, a compass, your usual diving gear – I can't think of anything else. Oh, a flashlight – you won't be able to do the whole trip in the daytime.'

'I was going to leave around midnight, then I'll have the Moon for the first half of the way, and I'll hit the coast during daylight.'

'You seem to have worked it out pretty well,' said Mick with grudging admiration. He still hoped that the attempt would be unnecessary and that something would turn up. But if it did not, he would do all that he could to launch Johnny towards the distant mainland.

Because both boys, like everyone else on the island, had to help with urgent repair work, they could do little until nightfall. Even after darkness came, there were some jobs that continued by the soft light of kerosene lanterns, and it was not until very late in the evening that Johnny and Mick were able to complete their arrangements.

Luckily, no one saw them as they brought the little surfboard down to the harbour and launched it among the overturned and shattered boats. Equipment and harness were all attached. Only the dolphins were needed now – and the final, unavoidable reason for going.

Johnny handed the communicator bracelet to Mick.

'See if you can call them,' he said. 'I'm running up to the hospital. I won't be more than ten minutes.'

Mick took the bracelet and waded out into deeper water. The

fluorescent letters were clearly visible on the tiny keyboard, but he did not need them, for, like Johnny, he could use the instrument blindfold.

He sank down into the warm, liquid darkness and lay on the coral sand. For a moment he hesitated; if he wished, there was still time to stop Johnny. Suppose he did nothing with the communicator and then said that the dolphins had never turned up? The chances were that they wouldn't come, anyway.

No, he could not deceive his friend, even in a good cause, even to save him from risking his life. He could only hope that when Johnny called at the hospital he would hear that the Professor was now out of danger.

Wondering if he would be sorry for this all his life, Mick pressed the HELP! button and heard the faint buzzing in the darkness. He waited fifteen seconds, then pressed it again – and again.

For his part, Johnny had no doubts. As he followed the beam of his flashlight up the beach and along the path to the administration centre, he knew that he might be setting foot on Dolphin Island for the very last time; that, indeed, he might not live to see another sunrise. This was a burden which few boys of his age had had to bear, but he accepted it willingly. He did not think of himself as a hero; he was merely doing his plain duty. He had been happy here on the island and had found a way of life that gave him everything he needed. If he wanted to preserve that way of life, he would now have to fight for it – and, if necessary, risk losing it.

The small hospital building, in which he himself had wakened as a sun-burned castaway a year ago, was completely silent. Curtains were drawn on all the windows except one, from which streamed the yellow light of a kerosene lamp. Johnny could not help glancing into the brightly illuminated room; it was the office, and Nurse Tessie was sitting at her desk. She was writing in a large register, or diary, and she looked completely exhausted. Several times she put her hands to her eyes, and Johnny was shaken to realize that she had been crying. The knowledge that this huge, capable woman had been reduced to tears was proof enough that the situation was desperate. Perhaps, he thought with a sudden sinking of his heart, he was already too late.

It was not as bad as that, though it was bad enough. Nurse cheered up a little, putting on her professional face when he knocked softly and entered the office. She would probably have thrown out anyone else who bothered her at this time of night, but she had always had a soft spot in her heart for Johnny.

'He's very ill,' she said in a whisper. 'With the right drugs, I could clear it up in a few hours. But as it is . . .' She shrugged her massive shoulders helplessly, then added, 'It's not only the Professor; I've two other patients who should have anti-tetanus shots.'

'If we don't get help,' whispered Johnny, 'do you think he'll pull through?'

She did not answer; her silence was enough, and Johnny waited no longer. Luckily, she was too tired to notice that he did not say good-night, but good-bye.

When Johnny got back to the beach, he found that Susie was already harnessed to the surf-board, and Sputnik was waiting patiently beside her.

'They got here in five minutes,' said Mick. 'Gave me a fright, too, when they came up in the darkness – I wasn't expecting them so soon.'

Johnny stroked the two wetly gleaming bodies, and the dolphins rubbed affectionately against him. He wondered where and how they had ridden out the storm, for he could not imagine any creature surviving in the seas that must have raged around the island. There was a cut behind Sputnik's dorsal fin that had not been there before, but otherwise neither dolphin seemed any the worse for its experience.

Water flask, compass, flashlight, sealed food-container, flippers, face-mask, snorkel, communicator – Johnny checked them all. Then he said, 'Thanks for everything, Mick – I'll be back soon.'

'I still wish I could go with you,' Mick answered huskily.

'There's nothing to worry about,' said Johnny, though he no longer felt quite so sure. 'Sputnik and Susie will look after me, won't you?' He could think of no more to say, so he climbed on to the board, called 'Let's go,' and waved to the disconsolate Mick as Susie pulled him out to sea.

He had made it just in time, for he could see lanterns moving down the beach. As he slipped away into the night, he felt sorry that he had left Mick to face the music.

Perhaps from this very beach, a century and a-half ago, Mary Watson had set off in her ill-fated bid for rescue, floating in that tiny iron box with her baby and dying servant. How strange it was that in this age of spaceships and atomic energy and colonies on the planets, he should be doing almost the same thing, from the same island!

Yet perhaps it was not so strange, after all. If he had never heard of her example, he might not have been inspired to repeat it. And if he succeeded, she would not have died in vain, on that lonely reef forty miles to the north.

Twenty

Johnny was content to let the dolphins do all the navigating until he was well clear of the reef. Their wonderful sonar system, filling the dark sea with echoes beyond his hearing, told them exactly where they were. It revealed to them all the obstacles and all the larger fish for a hundred feet around. Millions of years before men invented radar, dolphins (as well as bats) had perfected it in almost every detail. True, they used sound waves and not radio waves, but the principle was the same.

The sea was choppy, but not too rough. Sometimes spray would break over him, and occasionally the board would nose down into a wave, but most of the time he skimmed comfortably across the surface. It was difficult to judge his speed in the darkness. When he switched on his flashlight, the water seemed to be racing past him at a tremendous rate, but he knew that it could not be much more than ten miles an hour.

Johnny looked at his watch. Fifteen minutes had already passed, and when he glanced back, there was no sign of the island. He had expected to see a few lights, but even these were gone. Already he was miles from land, racing through the night on a mission that would have terrified him only a year ago. Yet he was unafraid – or at least he could control his fears, for he knew that he was with friends who would protect him from harm.

It was time he set his course. Navigation was no problem. If he travelled even approximately west, he was bound to hit somewhere on the thousands of miles of Australian coastline, sooner or later. When he glanced at his compass, he saw, to his surprise, that there was no need to make any change of direction. Susie was already on course, heading due west.

It was the clearest and most direct proof of her intelligence that he had ever received. Mick's 'HELP!' signal had been enough. There was no need to point to the one direction in which help could be found; she already knew it, as she probably knew every inch of the Queensland coastline.

But was she travelling as swiftly as she could? Johnny wondered whether to leave that to her, or whether to impress upon her the urgency of the mission. Finally he decided that it would do no harm to press the FAST button.

He felt the board jerk slightly when he did so, but he could not tell whether there had been any appreciable increase in speed. The hint should be sufficient. He was sure now that Susie knew exactly what she was was doing and was operating at her best cruising speed. If he insisted that she go faster, she would only tire herself.

The night was very dark, for the Moon had not yet risen, and low clouds left behind by the storm hid almost all the stars. Even the usual phosphorescence of the sea was absent; perhaps the luminous creatures of the deep were still recovering from the impact of the hurricane and would not shine again until they had got over their shock. Johnny would have welcomed their gentle radiance, for there were moments when he felt scared by this headlong race through pitch-black darkness. Suppose a huge wave – or even a rock – was rearing up invisibly ahead of him as he skimmed along with his nose only three inches from th · water? Despite his faith in Susie, these fears crept up on him from time to time, and he had to fight them down.

It was a wonderful moment when he saw the first pale glow of moonrise in the east. The clouds were still thick, but though he could not see the Moon itself, its reflected light began to grow around him. It was too faint to show any details; but merely to see the horizon made a great difference to his peace of mind. Now he could tell with his own eyes that there were no rocks or reefs ahead. Susie's underwater senses were far keener than his straining vision, but at least he was no longer completely helpless.

Now that they were in deeper water, the annoying, choppy wavelets over which the board had bumped at the beginning of its journey had been left behind. Instead, they were skimming across long, rolling waves, hundreds of feet from crest to crest. It was hard to judge their height; from Johnny's prone position, they doubtless seemed much bigger than they really were. Half the time, Susie would be climbing up a long, gentle slope; then the board would hover for an instant on the summit of the moving hill of water; then there would be the swoop down into the valley – then the whole sequence would begin again. Johnny had long since learned to adjust himself to the climb and the swoop, shifting his weight automatically along the board. Like riding a bicycle, he did it without conscious thought.

Suddenly the Moon's waning crescent broke through the clouds. For the first time, Johnny could see the miles of rolling water around him, the great waves marching endlessly into the night. Their crests gleamed like silver in the moonlight, making their troughs all the blacker by contrast. The surf-board's dive down into the dark valleys and its slow climb to the peaks of the moving hills were a continual switching from night to day, day to night.

Johnny looked at his watch; he had been travelling about four hours. That meant, with any luck, forty miles, and it also meant that dawn could not be far away. That would help him to fight off sleep. Twice he had dozed, fallen off the board, and found himself spluttering in the sea. It was not a pleasant feeling, floating there in the darkness while he waited for Susie to circle back and pick him up.

Slowly the eastern sky lightened. As he looked back, waiting for the first sight of the sun, Johnny remembered the dawn he had watched from the wreckage of the *Santa Anna*. How helpless he had felt then, and how mercilessly the tropical sun had burned him! Now he was calm and confident, though he had reached the point of no return, with fifty miles of sea separating him from land in either direction. And the sun could no longer harm him, for it had already tanned his skin a deep golden brown.

The swift sunrise shouldered away the night, and as he felt the warmth of the new day on his back, Johnny pressed the STOP button. It was time to give Susie a rest and a chance to go hunting for her breakfast. He slipped off the surf-board, swam forward, loosened her harness – and away she went, jumping joyfully in the air as she was released. There was no sign of Sputnik; he was probably chasing fish somewhere else, but would come quickly enough when he was called.

Johnny pushed up his face-mask, which he had worn all night to keep the spray out of his eyes, and sat astride the gently rocking board. A banana, two meat rolls, and a sip of orange juice was all he needed to satisfy him; the rest could wait until later in the day. Even if everything went well, he still had five or six hours of travelling ahead of him.

He let the dolphins have a fifteen-minute break while he relaxed on the board, rising and falling in the swell of the waves. Then he pressed the call button and waited for them to return.

After five minutes, he began to get a little worried. In that time they could swim three miles; surely they had not gone so far away? Then he relaxed as he saw a familiar dorsal fin cutting through the water towards him.

A second later, he sat up with a jerk. *That* fin was certainly familiar, but it was not the one he was expecting. It belonged to a killer whale.

Those few moments, as Johnny saw sudden death bearing down at thirty knots, seemed to last forever. Then a faintly reassuring thought struck him, and he dared to hope. The whale had almost certainly been attracted by his signal; could it possibly be . . .?

It was. As the huge head surfaced only a few feet away, he recognized the streamlined box of the control unit, still anchored securely in the massive skull.

'You gave me quite a shock, Snowy,' he said when he had recovered his breath. 'Please don't do that again.'

Even now, he had no guarantee of safety. According to the last reports, Snowy was still on an exclusive diet of fish; at least, there had been no complaints from the dolphins. But he was not a dolphin, nor was he Mick.

The board rocked violently as Snowy rubbed herself against it, and it was all that Johnny could do to keep himself from being thrown into the water. But it was a gentle rub – the gentlest that fifteen feet of killer whale could manage – and when she turned to repeat the manoeuvre on the other side, Johnny felt a good deal better. There was no doubt that she only wanted to be friendly, and he breathed a silent but fervent 'thank you' to Mick.

Still a little shaken, Johnny reached out and patted her as she slid by, so silently and effortlessly. Her skin had the typical, rubbery dolphin feel – which, of course, was natural enough. It was easy to forget that this terror of the seas was just another dolphin, only on a slightly bigger scale.

She seemed to appreciate Johnny's rather nervous stroking of her flank, for she came back for more.

'I guess you must be lonely, all by yourself,' said Johnny sympathetically. Then he froze in utter horror.

Snowy wasn't by herself, and she had no need to be lonely. Her boyfriend was making a leisurely approach – all thirty feet of him.

Only a male killer had that enormous dorsal fin, taller than a man. The huge black triangle, like the sail of a boat, came slowly up to the surf-board upon which Johnny was sitting, quite unable to move. All he could think was, '*You've* had no conditioning – no friendly swimming with Mick.'

This was far and away the largest animal that he had ever seen – it looked as big as a boat – and Snowy had suddenly shrunk to dolphin size by contrast. But she was the master – or mistress – of the situation, for as her huge mate patrolled slowly around the board, she circled on an inner orbit, always keeping between him and Johnny.

Once he stopped, reared his head a good six feet out of the water, and stared straight at Johnny across Snowy's back. There was hunger, intelligence, and ferocity in those eyes – or so it seemed to Johnny's heightened imagination – but no trace of friendliness. And all the time he was spiralling in towards the surf-board; in a very few minutes he would be squeezing Snowy against it.

Snowy, however, had other ideas. When her companion was only ten feet away and filling the whole of Johnny's field of view, she suddenly turned on him and gave him a nudge amidships. Johnny could hear the 'thump' clearly through the water; the impact would have been enough to stave in the side of a small boat.

The big whale took the gentle hint, and to Johnny's vast relief began to move farther outwards. Fifty feet away there was another slight disagreement, and another thump. That was the end of it. Within minutes, Snowy and her escort had vanished from sight, heading due north. As he watched them go, Johnny realized that he had just seen a ferocious monster converted into a hen-pecked husband, forbidden to take snacks between meals. The snack concerned was devoutly grateful.

For a long time, Johnny sat on the board, trying to regain control of his nerves. He had never been so scared in his life, and he was not ashamed of it, for he had had plenty to be scared about. But at last he stopped looking over his shoulder every few seconds to see what was coming up from behind, and began to get organized. The first order of business was: Where were Susie and Sputnik?

There had been no sign of them, and Johnny was not surprised. Undoubtedly, they had detected the killers and had wisely kept their distance. Even if they trusted Snowy, they would know better than to come near her mate.

Had they been scared completely away, or – horrible thought – had the killers already caught them? If they did not return, Johnny knew that he was finished, for he must still be at least forty miles from the Australian coast.

He was afraid to press the calling button a second time; it might bring back the killer whales, and he had no wish to go through *that* again, even if he could be sure that it would have the same happy ending. There was nothing he could do but sit and wait, scanning the sea around him for the first sign of a reasonable-sized dorsal fin, not more than a foot high.

Fifteen endless minutes later, Sputnik and Susie came swimming up from the south. They probably had been waiting for the coast to clear. Johnny had never been so pleased to see any humans as he was to greet the two dolphins. As he slipped off the board to fix the harness, he gave them the little pats and caresses they enjoyed, and talked to them just as if they could understand him. As, indeed, they certainly did, for though they knew only a few words of English, they were very sensitive to his tone of voice. They could always tell when he was pleased or angry, and now they must surely share his own feeling of overwhelming relief.

He tightened the buckles of Sputnik's harness, checked that blowhole and flippers were clear of the straps, and climbed back on to the board. As soon as he was lying flat and properly balanced, Sputnik started to move.

This time he did not continue westward towards Australia; instead, he headed south. 'Hey!' said Johnny. 'That's the wrong direction!' Then he thought of the killer whales and realized that this was not such a bad idea after all. He would let Sputnik have his head and see what happened.

They were going faster than Johnny had ever travelled on the board before. Speed so close to the water was very deceptive, but he would not be surprised if they were doing fifteen knots. Sputnik kept it up for twenty minutes; then, as Johnny had hoped and expected, they turned west. With any luck now, it would be a clear run to Australia.

From time to time he glanced back to see if they were followed, but no tall dorsal fin broke the emptiness behind them. Once, a big manta ray leaped clear out of the sea a few hundred yards away, hung in the air for a second like an enormous black bat, then fell back with a crash that could have been heard for miles. It was the only sign of the ocean's teeming life that he saw on the second lap of his journey.

Towards mid-morning, Sputnik began to slacken, but continued to pull gamely. Johnny was anxious not to halt again until the coast was in sight; then he intended to switch back to Susie, who would have had a good rest by that time. If his guesses of speed were correct, Australia could not be much more than ten miles away, and should be appearing at any moment.

He remembered how he had first glimpsed Dolphin Island, in circumstances which were so similar – yet so different. It had been like a small cloud on the horizon, trembling in the heat-haze. What he was approaching now was no island but a vast continent with a coastline thousands of miles long. Even the worst navigator could hardly miss such a target – and he had two of the best. He had not the slightest worry on this score, but he was getting a little impatient.

His first glimpse of the coast came when an unusually large roller lifted the surf-board. He glanced up, without thinking, when he was poised for a moment on the crest of the wave. And there, far ahead, was a line of white, stretching the full length of the horizon . . .

His breath caught in his throat, and he felt the blood pounding in his cheeks. Only an hour or two away was safety for himself and help for the Professor. His long sleigh-ride across the ocean was nearly over.

Thirty minutes later, a bigger wave gave him a better view of the coast ahead. And then he knew that the sea had not yet finished playing with him, his worst ordeal was still to come.

Twenty-one

The hurricane had passed two days ago, but the sea still remembered it. As he neared the coast, Johnny could make out individual trees and houses, and the faint blue humps of the inland hills. He also saw and heard the tremendous waves ahead. Their thunder filled the air; all along the coast, from north to south, white-capped mountains were moving against the land. The great waves were breaking a thousand feet out, as they hit the shelving beach. Like a man tripping and falling, they gained speed as they toppled, and when they finally crashed, they left behind them smoking clouds of spray.

Johnny looked in vain for a break somewhere along those moving, thundering walls of water. But as far as he could see – and when he stood up on the board, he could see for miles – the whole coastline was the same. He might waste hours hunting along it for sheltered bays or river mouths where he could make a safe landfall. It would be best to go straight through, and to do it quickly before he lost his nerve.

He had with him the tool for the job, but he had never used it. The hard, flat coral so close to shore made surf-riding impossible at Dolphin Island; there was no gentle underwater slope up which the breakers could come rolling into land. But Mick had often talked enthusiastically to him about the technique of 'catching a wave', and it did not sound too difficult. You waited out where the waves were beginning to break, then paddled like mad when you saw one coming up behind you. Then all you had to do was to hang onto the board and pray that you wouldn't get dumped. The wave would do the rest.

Yes, it sounded simple enough – but could he manage it? He

remembered that silly joke: 'Can you play the violin?' 'I don't know – I've never tried.' Failure here could have much more serious consequences than a few sour notes.

Half a mile from land, he gave Susie the signal to halt and unbuckled her harness. Then, very reluctantly, he cut the traces from the board; it would not do to have them whipping around him when he went barrelling through the surf. He had put a lot of work into that harness, and hated to throw it away. But he remembered Professor Kazan's remark: 'Equipment can always be replaced.' It was a source of danger now, and it would have to go.

The two dolphins still swam beside him as he paddled to-wards the shore, kicking the board along with his flippered feet, but there was nothing they could do to help him now. Johnny wondered if, superb swimmers though they were, they could even help themselves in the boiling maelstrom ahead. Dolphins were often stranded on beaches such as this, and he did not want Susie and Sputnik to run that risk.

This looked a good place to go in: the breakers were run-ning parallel to the beach without any confusing cross-patterns of reflected waves. And there were people here, watching the surf from the tops of some low sand dunes. Perhaps they had seen him already; in any case, they would be able to help him to get ashore.

He stood up on the board and waved vigorously – no easy feat on such an unstable platform. Yes, they'd seen him; those distant figures had suddenly become agitated, and several were pointing in his direction.

Then Johnny noticed something that did not make him at all happy. Up there on the dunes were at least a dozen surf-boards, some resting on trailers, some stuck upright in the sand. All those boards on land – and not a single one in the sea! Johnny knew, for Mick had told him often enough, that the

Australians were the best swimmers and surfers in the world. There they were, waiting hopefully with all their gear, but they knew better than to try anything in *this* sea. It was not an encouraging sight for someone about to attempt his first shoot.

He paddled slowly forward, and the roaring ahead grew steadily louder. Until now, the waves that swept past him had been smooth and unbroken, but now their crests were flecked with white. Only a hundred yards in front of him they would start to topple and fall thundering towards the beach, but here he was still in the safe no man's land between the breakers and the sea. Somewhere a fathom or two beneath him, the advancing waves, which had marched unhindered across a thousand miles of the open Pacific, first felt the tug and drag of the land. After that, they had only seconds left to live before they crashed in tumultuous ruin upon the beach.

For a long time, Johnny rose and fell at the outer edge of the white water, studying the behaviour of the waves, noting where they began to break, feeling their power without yielding to it. Once or twice he almost launched himself forward, but instinct or caution held him back. He knew – his eyes and ears told him plainly enough – that once he was committed, there would be no second chance.

The people on the beach were becoming more and more excited. Some of them were waving him back, and this struck him as very stupid. Where did they *expect* him to go? Then he realized that they were trying to help – they were warning him against waves that he should not attempt to catch. Once, when he almost started paddling, the distant watchers waved him frantically onward, but he lost his nerve at the last second. When he saw the wave that he had missed go creaming smoothly up the beach, he knew that he should have taken their advice. They were the experts; they understood this coast. Next time, he would do what they suggested.

He kept the board aimed accurately towards the land while he looked back over his shoulder at the incoming waves. Here was one that was already beginning to break as it humped out of the sea; whitecaps of foam had formed all along its crest. Johnny glanced quickly at the shore and caught a glimpse of dancing figures wildly waving him onward. This was it.

He forgot everything else as he dog-paddled with all his strength, urging the board up to the greatest speed that he could manage. It seemed to respond very sluggishly, so that he was barely crawling along the water. He dared not look back, but he knew that the wave was rising swiftly behind him, for he could hear its roar growing closer and louder every second.

Then it gripped the board, and his furious paddling became as useless as it was unnecessary. He was in the power of an irresistible force, so overwhelming that his puny efforts could neither help nor hinder it. He could only accept it.

His first sensation, when the wave had taken him, was one of surprising calm; the board felt almost as steady as if moving on rails. And though this was surely an illusion, it even seemed to have become quiet, as if he had left the noise and tumult behind. The only sound of which he was really conscious was the seething hiss of the foam as it boiled around him, frothing over his head so that he was completely blinded. He was like a bareback rider on a runaway horse, unable to see anything because its mane was streaming in his face.

The board had been well designed, and Johnny had a good sense of balance; his instincts kept him poised on the wave. Automatically, he moved backward or forward by fractions of an inch, to adjust his trim and to keep the board level, and presently he found that he could see again. The line of foam had retreated amidships; his head and shoulders were clear of the whistling, blinding spray, and only the wind was blowing in his face.

As well it might be, for he was surely moving at thirty or forty miles an hour. Not even Susie or Sputnik – not even Snowy – could match the speed at which he was travelling now. He was balanced on the crest of a wave so enormous that he would not have believed it possible; it made him giddy to look down into the trough beneath.

The beach was scarcely a hundred yards away, and the wave was beginning to curl over, only a few seconds before its final collapse. This, Johnny knew, was the moment of greatest danger. If the wave fell upon him now, it would pound him to pulp against the sea-bed.

Beneath him, he felt the board beginning to seesaw – to tilt nose down in that sickening plunge that would end everything. The wave he was riding was deadlier than any monster of the sea – and immeasurably more powerful. Unless he checked this forward lurch, he would slide down the curving cliff of water, while the unsupported overhang of the wave grew larger and larger, until at last it came crashing down upon him.

With infinite care, he eased his weight back along the board, and the nose slowly lifted. But he dared not move too far back, for he knew that if he did so he would slide off the shoulders of this wave and be left for the one behind to pulverize. He had to keep in exact, precarious balance, on the very peak of this mountain of foam and fury.

The mountain was beginning to sink beneath him, and he sank with it, still holding the board level as it flattened into a hill. Then it was only a mound of moving foam, all its strength stolen from it by the braking action of the beach. Through the now aimless swirl of foam, the board still darted forward, coasting like an arrow under its own momentum. Then there came a sudden jolt, a long snaky slither – and Johnny found himself looking not at moving water but at motionless sand.

At almost the same instant he was grabbed by firm hands and

hoisted to his feet. There were voices all around him, but he was still deafened by the roar of the sea and heard only a few scattered phrases like, 'Crazy young fool – lucky to be alive – not one of *our* kids.'

'I'm all right,' he muttered, shaking himself free.

Then he turned back, wondering if he could see any sign of Sputnik and Susie beyond the breakers. But he forgot all about them in that shattering moment of truth.

For the first time, as he stared at the mountainous waves storming and smoking towards him, he saw what he had ridden through. This was something that no man could hope to do twice; he was indeed lucky to be alive.

Then his legs turned to water as the reaction hit him, and he was thankful to sit down, clutching with both hands at the firm, welcoming Australian soil.

Twenty-two

'You can go in now,' said Nurse Tessie. 'But only five minutes, remember. He's not very strong yet, and he hasn't quite got over his last visitor.'

Johnny knew all about that. Two days before, Mrs Kazan had descended upon the island 'like a troop of Cossacks', as someone had said with only slight exaggeration. She had made a vigorous attempt to whisk the Professor back to Moscow for treatment, and it had taken all of Tessie's determination and the Professor's wiliness to frustrate her. Even then they might have been defeated, but, luckily, the doctor who flew over from the mainland every day had given strict orders that his patient must not be moved for at least a week. So Mrs Kazan had left for Sydney, to see what Australia could offer in the way of culture – which was now a very great deal. She would be back, she promised, in exactly one week.

Johnny tiptoed into the sick-room. At first he could hardly see Professor Kazan, who was lying in bed entirely surrounded by books, quite unaware that he had company. It was at least a minute before the Professor noticed his visitor, then he hurriedly put down the book he was reading and extended his hand in welcome.

'I'm so pleased to see you, Johnny; thank you for everything. You took a very big risk.'

Johnny made no attempt to deny it. The risk had been far greater than he had dreamed when he had set out from Dolphin Island a week ago. Perhaps if he had known . . . But he had done it, and that was all that mattered.

'I'm glad I went,' he answered simply.

'So am I,' said the Professor. 'Nurse says the Red Cross 'copter was just in time.'

There was a long, awkward silence. Then Professor Kazan went on, in a lighter tone.

'How did you like the Queenslanders?'

'Oh, they're wonderful people – though it was a long time before they'd believe I came from Dolphin Island.'

'I'm not surprised,' said the Professor dryly. 'And what did you do while you were over there?'

'Well, I can't remember how many television and radio broadcasts I had to make – I got rather fed up with them. But the best part was the surf-riding; when the sea was calmer, they took me out and really showed me all the tricks. I'm now,' he added with pride, 'an Honorary Life Member of the Queensland Surf Club.'

'That's fine,' answered the Professor, a little absently. It was obvious to Johnny that he had something on his mind, and presently he brought it out.

'Now, Johnny,' he said, 'I've had time to do a lot of thinking these last few days while I've been lying here. And I've come to a good many decisions.'

That sounded faintly ominous, and Johnny wondered what was coming next.

'In particular,' continued the Professor, 'I've been worrying about your future. You're seventeen now, and it's time you looked ahead.'

'You know that I want to stay here, Professor,' said Johnny in some alarm. 'All my friends are on the island.'

'Yes, I know that. But there's the important matter of your education; OSCAR can take you only part of the way. If you want to do anything useful, you'll have to specialize and develop whatever talents you have. Don't you agree?'

'I suppose so,' Johnny answered, without enthusiasm. Where was all this leading? he wondered.

'What I'm suggesting,' said the Professor, 'is that we get you into the University of Queensland next semester. Don't look so upset – it's not the other side of the world. Brisbane's only an hour from here, and you can get back any week end. But you can't spend *all* your life skin-diving around the reef!'

Johnny decided that he would be quite willing to try, but in his heart he knew that the Professor was right.

'You have skills and enthusiasms we need badly,' said Professor Kazan. 'What you still lack is discipline and knowledge – and you'll get both at the University. Then you'll be able to play a big part in the plans I have for the future.'

'What plans?' asked Johnny, a little more hopefully.

'I think you know most of them. They all add up to this – mutual aid between men and dolphins, to the advantage of both. In the last few months we've found some of the things we can do together, but that's only a feeble beginning. Fish-herding, pearl-diving, rescue operations, beach patrols, wreck surveys, water sports – oh, there are hundreds of ways that dolphins can help us! And there are much bigger things ...'

For a moment, he was tempted to mention that sunken spaceship, lost back in the Stone Age. But he and Keith had decided to say nothing about that until they had more definite information; it was the Professor's ace in the hole, not to be played until the right moment. One day, when he felt that it was time to increase his budget, he was going to try that piece of dolphin mythology on the Space Administration and wait for the dollars to roll in ...

Johnny's voice interrupted his reverie.

'What about the killer whales, Professor?'

'That's a long-term problem, and there's no simple answer to it at the moment. Electrical conditioning is only one of the tools we'll have to use, when we've decided on the best policy. But I think I know the final solution.'

He pointed to the low table at the other side of the room.

'Bring over that globe, Johnny.'

Johnny carried across the twelve-inch globe of the Earth, and the Professor spun it on its axis.

'Look here,' he said. 'I've been thinking about Reservations – Dolphins Only, Out of Bounds to Killer Whales. The Mediterranean and the Red Sea are the obvious places to start. It would take only about a hundred miles of fencing to seal them off from the oceans and to make them quite safe.'

'Fencing?' asked Johnny incredulously.

The Professor was enjoying himself. Despite Nurse's warning, he looked quite capable of going on for hours.

'Oh, I don't mean wire-netting or any solid barrier. But when we know enough Orcan to talk to killer whales, we can use underwater sound projectors to shepherd them around and keep them out of places where we don't want them to go. A few speakers in the Straits of Gibraltar, a few in the Gulf of Aden – that will make two seas safe for dolphins. And later, perhaps we can fence off the Pacific from the Atlantic, and give one ocean to the dolphins and the other to the killer whales. See, it's not far from Cape Horn to the Antarctic, the Bering Strait's easy, and only the gap south of Australia will be hard to close. The whaling industry's been talking about this sort of operation for years, and sooner or later it's going to be done.'

He smiled at the rather dazed look on Johnny's face, and came back to earth.

'If you think that half my ideas are crazy, you're quite right. But we don't know *which* half, and that's what we've got to find out. Now do you understand why I want you to go to college? It's for my own selfish reasons, as well as your own good.'

Before Johnny could do more than nod in reply, the door opened.

'I said five minutes, and you've taken ten,' grumbled Nurse Tessie. 'Out you go. And here's your milk, Professor.'

Professor Kazan said something in Russian which conveyed, quite clearly, the impression that he didn't like milk. But he was already drinking it by the time that Johnny, in a very thoughtful mood, had left the room.

He walked down to the beach, along the narrow path that wound through the forest. Most of the fallen trees had been cleared away, and already the hurricane seemed like a nightmare that could never really have happened.

The tide was in, covering most of the reef with a sheet of water nowhere more than two or three feet deep. A gentle breeze was playing across it, producing the most curious and beautiful effects. In some areas the water was flat and oily, still as the surface of a mirror. But in others it was corrugated into billions of tiny ripples, sparkling and twinkling like jewels as their ever changing curves reflected the sunlight.

The reef was lovely and peaceful now, and for the last year it had been his whole world. But wider worlds were beckoning; he must lift his eyes to farther horizons.

He no longer felt depressed by the prospect of the years of study still ahead. That would be hard work, but it would also be a pleasure; there were so many things he wanted to learn about the Sea.

And about its People, who were now his friends.

A note from the author

Dolphin Island was written in 1962, while I was recovering from the near-fatal accident described in two of my other books, *The Treasure of the Great Reef* and *The View from Serendip*. At the time I was still almost paralysed and never imagined I would ever be able to dive again; I wrote the book as a conscious farewell to the sea – which, I am happy to say, turned out to be premature. A year later I was back in the Indian Ocean . . . though I had no business being there, since I was not yet strong enough to stand upright whilst wearing an aqualung. But with the sea-bed only five metres below carpeted with silver, it was difficult to obey the dictates of commonsense.

During the last fifteen years dolphins have inspired a huge literature – not to mention a television series and several films. Many of the ideas in this book are therefore more familiar than they were back in 1962; however, we are still almost completely in the dark about the *real* intelligence of dolphins, and their larger cousins, the whales. They certainly possess some kind of 'language', and the famous record *The Songs of the Humpbacked Whale* has demonstrated that birds are very amateurish music-makers compared with the 'people of the sea'.

In 1962 I thought I was going out on a limb by suggesting that men could ever share the water with such powerful and dangerous animals as killer whales. Now men *and* women have swum with them, and even ridden on their backs; these whales have become favourite exhibits in the world's oceanariums. Their terrifying reputation appears to be a myth, for they have never been known to harm human beings – though they certainly have every excuse for doing so!

In 1970 I was able to achieve one of my ambitions by swimming with a dolphin in the open sea, off Hawaii. My companion, Li-Li, was the first dolphin ever to be trained to come back on command, answering to underwater sound signals. Since then dolphins have been used on many occasions (e.g. by the US Navy) to recover objects lost on the sea-bed. It is very likely that they will be valued assistants in our coming exploitation of the ocean's enormous wealth.

The controlling of animals by electrical impulses fed into their brains, as described in Chapter 16, is now a well-known fact; one brave scientist has done so in the bull-ring, stopping a charging bull a few metres away from him! In *Tales from the White Hart* I suggested trying this technique on one of the largest, strangest and most intelligent of all the sea's inhabitants – the near-legendary giant squid.

All the descriptions of the Great Barrier Reef, both above and below the water, are entirely factual and are based on my own explorations as described in *The Coast of Coral*. The story of Mary Watson in Chapter 13 is perfectly true, and I have changed neither names nor dates. However, her tragic adventure occurred not on my imaginary Dolphin Island, but on Lizard Island, much nearer to the mainland. The full story, with a reproduction of Mary Watson's diary (which I have held in my own hands) will be found in *The Coast of Coral*.

I would like to express my thanks to Mr F. G. Wood, then Curator of Marineland, Florida, for much valuable information on dolphins and other marine mammals. The description of underwater ultra-violet fluorescence in Chapter 18 is based on my own experience in the Indian Ocean with a watertight u.v. lamp, generously provided by Dr Richard G. Woodbridge of Trans-space Laboratories, who pioneered this field of submarine illumination.

London, April 1977